Also by Domenic Stansberry

Chasing the Dragon

Manifesto for the Dead

The Last Days of Il Duce

The Confession

The Spoiler

THE BIG BOO

the BIG BOOM

Domenic Stansberry

St. Martin's Minotaur New York

 For information, address St. Martin's Press, 175 Fifth Avenue, New York, N.Y. 10010.

www.minotaurbooks.com

Library of Congress Cataloging-in-Publication Data

Stansberry, Domenic.
The big boom / Domenic Stansberry.—1st ed.
p. cm.
ISBN-13: 978-0-312-32470-4
ISBN-10: 0-312-32470-7
1. North Beach (San Francisco, Calif.)—Fiction. 2. Police, Private—Fiction. I. Title.

PS3569.T3335B54 2006
813'.54—dc22

2006041707

First Edition: May 2006

10 9 8 7 6 5 4 3 2 1

PART ONE

ONE

It was the time of the big boom and everyone figured the prosperity would last forever. There had been other booms before, but those had always been followed by calamity—a bust that took away everything the good times had given, then kept on taking. This boom would be different, people said. The Transamerica Pyramid at the end of Kearney seemed almost to glow, and the bankers who worked inside issued a stream of proofs and prognostications. Meanwhile the streets swelled with new arrivals. The old-timers found the new enthusiasm insufferable, but the old-timers found everything insufferable. The truth was, you could see a certain gleam in their eyes, too, and at night the streets along North Beach echoed with the sounds of pleasure: from Tosca's to the Café Sport to the old U.S. Restaurant. The lines were long and there was a restive, animal smell. Those with pressing reservations left their cars along Kearney, double-parked, to be fetched from impound in the morning by couriers who specialized in the service. Such behavior did not seem extravagant under the circumstances. The bounty of the moment was infinite, after all—if only you could reach out and extend your grasp.

Meanwhile it was still possible—strolling down Columbus, perhaps, or turning a corner on Grant—to meet the plaintive stare of someone not sharing in the general prosperity. Sometimes at night, alone on your mattress, you might hear a soft cry. If you went to the window, though—nothing.

Just the fog and the darkened row houses and the arc lamp casting its blue light on the corner.

It was possible to experience doubt at such moments, of course, even if you realized such doubts would inevitably give way in the morning to the knowledge that the old order was evaporating. That soon everything would be transformed. If you continued to doubt, all you had to do was glance at the Pyramid for reassurance. Or at the newspapers. Or at the people absorbed in their handheld devices. So, after a while, if you heard those soft cries at night, you did not go to the window. And walking the streets, you did not meet those plaintive glances. You did not notice. Just as no one noticed, this particular evening, the corpse floating in the water.

The corpse surfaced at the end of the pier, floating in the manner that corpses float, face down, arms dangling. The corpse wore a silk blouse, the pearls still about the neck, the skirt ballooning from the flesh.

There were a number of people out strolling, stopping at the railing, gazing at the bay, at the numinous reflections skittering across its black surface. But no one noticed the dark form in the water, or if they did, they did not attach to it any significance. Perhaps their eyes were focused on the distance, on the lights glittering on the horizon. Or perhaps on something within—some notion they could not quite possess.

Meanwhile, a steamer passed, and the corpse rocked with the swells, the head gently thudding against the pilings. Sometime in the morning, just as the sky was graying, the body submerged again, not wholly, but just enough to slip beneath the pier. The morning crowds came. They disembarked from the ferry, walked along the wooden planks, ate on the benches. The corpse floated beneath them, lodged on the piling, just out of view. A stench rose—masked in part by the water, it was true, by the smells of the bay—but no one went to look. Perhaps no one would have discovered it at all if not for a fisherman—a boy, really, a kid from the Chinatown projects—who two days later got his line, his favorite lure, tangled in the darkness beneath the pier.

TWO

It was late afternoon, and Dante Mancuso sat in the Serafina Café, lingering at the counter with the air of someone who had lingered here before. He had a newspaper spread in front of him, but he was no longer reading. His eyes were hooded, and there was in his expression something hidden.

Dante was in his late thirties—a man with aquiline features, wide lips, an immodest nose. The nose was a family trait. The crooked beak, the humped camel, the wriggly worm. The old Sicilians had had a hundred names for the promontory at the center of their faces. Dante had their dark eyes as well, and a quick smile. A smile that because of the sharpness of his features seemed somehow more tender, more vulnerable. A smile both tender and menacing.

But Dante was not smiling now. He was all nose.

He sat in the Serafina, empty plate to the side, with that nose pointed downward at the newspaper spread on the counter. On the inside page, there was a two-inch story with a simple headline.

CORPSE PULLED FROM BAY

Dante pushed the paper aside. The Serafina was a dark place, thick with the stench of the past—a little mom-and-pop joint tucked between Ling's Wei's Grocery and the Colombo Hotel. It was the kind of place people passed by in their search for the authentic North Beach. Serafina's was authentic enough, of course, but it didn't have the kind of authenticity people wanted. Rather its windows were sooty and the old Italian woman who owned the place was no Mona Lisa.

"I hate those people," Stella said, pointing to the stream of passersby. The glass was dark and the people strolling by, out there in the sunshine, seemed little more than shadows.

"Me, too," said old man Pesci.

Pesci was ancient, in his nineties, near blind, and wore a black shirt with a red rose stitched into the collar. His teeth were cigarette yellow, his eyes clouded. "I hate everyone."

"Of course you do," said George Marinetti.

Marinetti was trying to be agreeable. He was in his late seventies, some dozen-odd years younger than Pesci, and had not meant to stir things up. Even so, the older man shot him a look of disdain.

"Don't humor me," snapped Pesci. "I know what you're up to."

Marinetti looked to Dante then, as if he were the arbiter. In some way, Dante had played this role since he was young. He was the watcher, the audience: the one who listened to their stories. This particular argument was not new to him. Truth was, Marinetti had set things off, intentionally or not, by mentioning he might sell his place on Vallejo Street. His wife had died the year before, and Marinetti was having trouble with his knees, getting up the stairs. Still . . .

"No one has a spine anymore," said Stella. She had her hands on her hips and her breasts were out. "Everyone runs. They sell out, first chance they get."

"I've lived in the same flat sixty years," said Marinetti.

"That's nothing," said Pesci. "I remember . . . I goddamn remember . . ."

Old man Pesci, his head weak on its stem, made a vague gesture at the window, at the passing shadows. He blew smoke from his lungs and started to cough. It was a horrible, vicious cough. When it died down, you could hear the crowd passing outside. Anxious laughter. A burst of Chinese. Someone calling for a cab.

Marinetti turned to Dante, still looking for a way out.

"What are you reading, your nose in the paper?"

"The comics, the funny papers . . . ," Pesci said, interrupting. "What do you think he's reading, our man here, Mr. Investigator. Mr. Nose-in-Everyone's-Business."

Dante was an ex-cop, with a tangled history. He'd left the neighborhood for a while, but now he was back. He'd returned home some six months ago, after his father's death. Things had settled now and he was working with Jake Cicero, special cases, private investigation. They all knew this, of course. These Italians, they knew everything, talked to everybody. Probably they knew that Barbara and Nick Antonelli had been down to Jake Cicero's office yesterday.

Their daughter, Angela Antonelli, was missing.

Dante had known Angie as a little girl. There was a picture of the two of them together along here somewhere, yellowing under the counter glass—along with pictures of half the people in the neighborhood. Or the neighborhood as it had been.

Angie was seven years old in the picture, a brunette in her communion dress. Dante was twelve, standing alongside her outside the church. Dante had known her more intimately later on, in his twenties, in a way a man knows a woman. The old ones would know that as well, of course.

"It's good for business, that is one thing I will say," said Ernesto Mollini.

Mollini lit a cigarette. You weren't supposed to smoke in restaurants anymore, it was against all the ordinances, but no one paid any attention to that in Serafina's.

"What are you saying?" asked Stella. "What's good for business?"

"All these new people."

"What business you in, you could say such a thing?"

"I have eyes."

"The sitting-around business, that's you," Stella said. "Sit around and blow smoke out your ass."

Ernesto was used to her talk. He was a butcher, or he had been. His shop was around the corner—but his sons operated it now.

"Let's ask Dante," said Stella, turning to Dante. "What do you think here, Mr. Funny Pages? Is it a good time to sell?"

Any conversation with Stella was treacherous ground, but especially this ground. Dante knew what was underneath. After his father died, a rumor had gone around. *Dante is going to sell. He is going to marry Marilyn Visconti. She's in real estate now, the Visconti girl, working for Joe Prospero. Dante's going to marry her. They will sell his father's place and leave for good.*

But it hadn't happened yet, no. He hadn't married Marilyn and he hadn't left. Instead Dante had leased out his father's house on Fresno Street to some couple from back East and was living alone in an apartment over Columbus Avenue.

"Why you ask him? He has no opinion worth listening too," snorted Pesci. There was something like a gleam in his eye. "Otherwise, why would he be sitting around in here. He would be married. He would have himself a woman on the side, with skin like milk. He would have himself a big car and a house on the moon."

Outside, the shadows were still passing. It was a steady stream these days—people suffused with the energy of the new prosperity. Dante thought about the corpse in the bay. It was not fair, maybe, but he hoped the body belonged to one of those newcomers, a stranger he had elbowed past on the street without seeing, some face he could no longer remember.

The paper had given few details.

"It's time for me to sell," said Marinetti. "Look at all these people. I mean, the tree is heavy."

"Heavy with what?"

"The fruit is ripe."

"What kind of talk is this?"

"People need a place to live. Prices are through the roof."

"You know what happens, Mr. Greedy? You think you sell, you make a million dollars, you move to paradise? That's what you think?"

Stella had opinions on these matters. If no one had sold, then the neighborhood would be okay. If no one had sold, you would still have the Sicilians down by the wharf and the Luccans in the heights and the Calabrians working out at the cannery. There would still be opera out on the streets, and in the open-air markets you would hear the glorious Italian language, and the streets would be clean, and there would be grapevines growing up the telephone poles and beautiful brown-eyed kids on every corner. Julius Caesar would still be alive, and Mussolini, well . . .

"My son, he has never sold so many meatballs," said Ernesto Mollini.

"Meatballs," said Stella. "Fuck them and their meatballs."

"Every one of these new people—they want a Sicilian meatball."

"They will forget in two days. People like that—these new people, they chase the fashion. And anyway, they don't come to a place like this."

Stella said it with a mix of pride and bitterness, but she was right. Once upon a time, Serafina's had been the place. Back when her husband was still alive—her husband the anarchist, relative to Carlo Tresca—back then the bohemians and famosos had come to hunch around the table with the neighborhood types, the dock-workers and the fisherman and the produce hustlers and all the rest. But those days were gone—and since her husband's death, Stella's anarchism had turned reactionary. She had never really liked the bohos anyway.

"Well, I don't know," said Marinetti. "Probably I will stay where I am."

"You will sell," said Stella.

"What kind of thing is that to say?"

"My son saw you down at Prospero's real estate office," said Pesci. "You and your daughter. Talking with Marilyn Visconti. He saw you in there."

Marinetti said nothing.

"Anyway, it is not your decision," said Stella.

"What do you mean?"

"You will do what your daughter says."

"That's not true," said Marinetti. "I decide my life."

The truth, Dante knew, was something different. Marinetti was in a bind. He had signed power of attorney over to his daughter after his wife's death. The old man put on a front in public, but Marinetti was lonely and wept in the apartment. Also, he was running out of money—and if he sold the house he could afford to move into a home. Meanwhile his daughter and her bum husband needed their inheritance now.

"Children," he said suddenly. "They are nothing but a heartache."

The room went quiet. A wine-colored light intoxicated the air. Marinetti thinking about the two sons he'd lost, maybe. Ernesto about the family butcher shop that was slowly going under, meatballs or no. Stella about the son who'd moved to Italy, and the other who wouldn't speak to her, and a third who'd vanished, no one knew where. And Pesci reaching for his Pall Mall, thinking of nothing but his cigarette. For a minute Dante was tempted to look for all of their pictures under the glass, to see if they had ever been young. To look for himself and Angie as well. Then he remembered the corpse down at the morgue, and the task that lay ahead of him. He could turn down the case. He didn't have to go if he didn't want to, he told himself. He didn't have to do anything. *I'm selling.* He lit another cigarette. When he stood up, the others were looking at him, and he wondered if he had spoken aloud. Then Dante threw some money down on that counter glass, on all those fading photos, and went out to join the parade.

THREE

Unlike the living, who held their secrets within, the corpse had no shame. It no longer spoke in the language of the tongue, with all its limitations, but in the language of putrescence. Of stench and gastric fluids. Of unexpected gurgles and gaseous discharges. *Did you love me?* The medical coroner, as well as the detectives who had grappled the body from the bay, were familiar to some degree with the language of the dead, but their transliterations were not precise. They had their evidence kits, their test reagents, their sliced organs in plastic sacks, and their mass spectrometers—but these only told the investigators so much. There was too much noise in the field, so to speak: the rattle of their own lives, the hollering of spouses and children, the flushing of toilets, the sound of their own rumbling bellies. With so much interference, it was all but impossible to filter the noise from the message.

No, no. Look at me.

Nonetheless, there were things that could be determined. A woman in her early thirties. Four days in the water, maybe five. Traces of aspirated foam in her airways. Lungs bloated, chest distended. The medical examiner suspected death by drowning, though it was hard to be definitive in such instances. It was possible, too, the young woman had been dead before she went in. There were wounds to her head and extremities, but it was hard to tell what these meant. The corpse typically got battered as it was dragged along the bottom by the currents.

Don't let me go.

The skin was macerated on the finger pads, and her face and nose looked as if they had been abraded. The soft parts of the face had been eaten by crabs and bottom fish. The translucency was gone from the skin. The lividity was blotchy about the head and the chest—pink in places but already gone dusky and cyanotic in others. Decomposition had been slowed somewhat by the coldness of the bay, but the putrefaction advanced quickly once the body was in the open air. The clothes, sodden with water, were stripped away and placed in evidence bags.

A pleated skirt, label from Dazio's.

Black hose.

A pair of pumps. Purple.

A silk blouse.

Pearl necklace.

A scarf.

No wallet, though. No purse. No source of identification. The stripping of the clothes revealed more maceration, bloating of the limbs. Also bruises on the thighs and forearms—though again, whether these had occurred before death, or after, as the corpse thudded against the pier, was hard to tell. Examination of the vulva showed no signs of sexual penetration. Though again, this was hard to ascertain.

Fuck me.

All these details were written down, recorded in cramped forms to be followed by more reports from the pathologist. Whisperings of the dead, duly noted. If you read the hieroglyph correctly, it led to other documents, to a Missing Persons report, maybe, and eventually to an address. And inside that address were rooms, drawers filled with bills, papers, more scribblings, phone messages, all of which led to friends and family, if there were any, hence to conversations with the living, more hieroglyphs transliterated through memory and dreams.

Don't forget me.

In the morgue now, there was the sound of the refrigeration unit: then footsteps—and a long metal drawer sliding open on its rusted hinge. The bag was zippered opened and a man sighed, peering into the bag.

And maybe there was some vibration in the mass of cells there on the metal slab. Maybe there was something that connected the nerves to the cells to the fiber to the atrophying mass inside the plastic bag. Something that animated the swollen brain and the optic nerve and whatever was still sentient in that mass.

The man who peered in had a long nose and a sorrowful face and compassionate eyes. His looks had excited the corpse once upon a time, when it was not a corpse, when the bacteria that inhabited the animal were different bacteria and the energy congregated in a different way. The memory of him, or its chemical remains, lingered inside the flesh, and so his presence was recognized in some way. Or so the man imagined. He imagined the corpse peering out from the bag as he peered in.

In another minute he went away.

His footsteps receded, and then the corpse was slid back into the wall, into the cold and the dark.

Dante, the corpse whispered.

The voice was in his head, Dante told himself. It wasn't real. But such distinctions didn't matter. *Take me home.* Once it got inside of you, there it was. You had no choice but to listen. *Don't abandon me. Don't leave me here.*

FOUR

All his life, Dante's job had been to follow, to put his nose into things, and there were times when he felt he was being followed in turn—that he was being watched in the way that he himself watched others. It was a feeling not uncommon in his profession.

He had one of those feelings now—at the 280 merge, heading south, eight lanes of traffic coming together at once—and he watched the rearview all the way to San Mateo. There was no one there.

Truth was, the feeling never really left him. Habit. Survival instinct. Or the family paranoia, his mind coming loose at the hinge.

Late that afternoon, Dante met with Barbara and Nick Antonelli at their house down on the peninsula. Fifteen years ago, the Antonellis had sold their place on Russian Hill, and now they lived on a hillside in San Mateo, in a ranch house with colored gravel out front and a giant pumice rock in the courtyard. Dante recognized the rock; it was made of some volcanic material with a surface like cut glass. He had leaned against it, a long time ago, and the microscopic edges had sliced his palms.

Barbara Antonelli met him at the door. She was an elegant woman in her midfifties, a small-boned woman whose presence was in some ways more striking than her daughter's.

"Come in, Dante," she said. "Nick's on the phone. Some business thing. I— Can I get you something?"

Barbara had always liked him, Dante knew that. The same wasn't necessarily true of her husband. It had been a while since Dante had seen her, and though she had aged, of course, and it was apparent she was anxious, hollow-eyed with worry, she was still well dressed and had about her an air of glamour. She had the air of a woman who had a secret life and passionate feelings.

"Would you like a drink?"

There was something incongruous about the offer, but the everyday routines often seemed so at such times. The Antonellis had always been big on cocktails, Dante remembered. Given the circumstances, and the fact that he was on the job, Dante figured he should turn her down. But he didn't.

"What are you having?" he asked.

"What I always have," she smiled dimly. It was a vague smile, a little twist. Angie's smile. "A little gin, a little tonic. Lots of ice."

"Okay," he said. "That would be fine."

She went to the ice bucket they kept at the bar, and rattled around. Out in the back, behind her, were the swimming pool and the landscaped yard and the outdoor kitchen.

"It's been a long time," he said.

"Two weeks."

"No," he said, then realized his mistake. He had been making small talk, but she was thinking about how long since she'd last seen her daughter. When Barbara glanced at him now, he saw all the grief and the worry. Her gaze skittered away.

"I have to get some ice. We've been going through it lately."

She left the room, and he had a chance to look around. Grass mat wallpaper. An overstuffed coach. Slate on the fireplace, gray slate, gray and black—and in the corner a baby grand that no one played. On the grand was a photo of Angie. It was one of those studio shots, the kind that make people look stiff and fat-cheeked, but there were other pictures in the room, too. Angie on the porch of the old place on Russian Hill. Angie in high school. Angie, a few years back, at a friend's wedding. Angie with her mother's dirty blond hair and her freckled skin and those piercing eyes.

There'd been a moment fifteen years ago, when Dante had been in this same room—and Barbara Antonelli had come upon him unexpectedly. Her face had been raw with anger, but when she came upon Dante, the anger had dropped away, and there'd been something naked in the air between them, something that he could not put a name to, even now. Then her husband had walked in behind her.

Whispered in her ear.

Nick Antonelli was unfaithful. It was common knowledge, and Dante had known it, too, back then, same as everyone else.

Whatever it was Nick had whispered, leaning into her that day, Barbara Antonelli's face had gone crimson.

Now Barbara returned. She brought ice from the outdoor refrigerator, and her husband came with her. Nick Antonelli was a thickset guy with hair that was too black and uniform to be natural. He was close to sixty. He wore a white shirt with ribbing.

His arms were muscular. He was a cocksure guy, even now, but that didn't mean you couldn't see his vulnerability.

"Ah, Dante," he said. He spoke a bit too loudly and shook Dante's hand a bit too vigorously. He was appetitive, full of himself, and this was part of his charm. "Every time I see you I am reminded of your grandfather."

"So they say."

"Yes, but it's so true. Dom Pellicano—you are his spitting image."

"The Pelican," Dante said.

He'd heard the name a lot lately. It was his grandfather's nickname, and Dante's nickname, too, among the old-timers anyway, partly on account of the surname, of course. But more on account of his nose.

The snout. The dangling fish. The big banana.

"I remember your grandfather from when I was little boy. He was the same age you are now, close enough—same way of standing, his feet set apart." Dante knew the story, his grandfather climbing out of his boat down at the wharf—pulling the purse seine and hurling it onto the dock. Tenacious son of a bitch. Hardheaded bird who one day pulled a gun because the Luccans were trying to chase him off his fishing grounds.

"He looked so much like you. Same eyes. Same face. Same goddamn nose."

"The family monstrosity."

"It's a beautiful nose," protested Barbara.

"I don't know about that," said Nick. "I don't know if I'd call it beautiful."

"Nick . . . ," Barbara intervened.

"Oh, Dante understands. I'm just jealous. A nose like that."

Nose like Gibraltar. Nose like the Italian peninsula. Nose like the snout of Claretta Petacci's dog, sticking itself up Il Duce's ass.

Dante had mixed feelings toward Nick Antonelli. They'd been close once, for a little while. There was something infectious about the man, but he always had to get the best of you. He had to know more about everything. His family was old North Beach relatively speaking, but they weren't the gentry. They had come from Chicago, and there were stories about how his family had rough-handed their way into the local warehouse trade. Whatever the truth of the situation, Nick had built on what his father left him and made a little empire for himself in commercial property.

"So what have you found out about my daughter?"

Dante hesitated. He was not anxious to tell them about his trip to the morgue. "Cicero only just talked to me this morning," Dante said. "He just passed me his notes. I've done a few things . . . but before I do anything else, I wanted to see what you could tell me."

They went through the details then, and he heard firsthand what he'd already learned from Cicero: that Angie had been supposed to come to dinner last Sunday, but she hadn't showed up. She hadn't returned her calls. Then, Tuesday afternoon, Barbara had gone to her daughter's apartment on Green Street, at the foot of Russian Hill.

"The mail was starting to pile up. And the cat was loose—and it looked like she'd left right in the middle of things. But you know how she was."

Dante knew well enough. Angie could be impetuous. On the outside she had her mother's reserve, and some of her delicacy, the studied movement, the careful fingers that brushed back her hair with a certain decorum. But Angie's expressions were more changeable, her looks fresher, raw and wide-boned. In some ways she more resembled her father, her features animated by an inner light that burned a bit too feverishly.

"Did you contact *The Chronicle*?"

"No, no. She left there quite some time ago. She'd been working on her own, freelance, for a number of years—doing pretty well. Then she got this new position."

"With who?"

"It's a complicated thing. She was involved with Michael Solano, you know him?"

"No."

"Well, I didn't either—but it seems everybody else does." She glanced at her husband with a look that Dante did not quite get, then went on. "Michael Solano's one of those new entrepreneurs, those people who are going to change the world, and he's on those lists of most eligibles, in the society columns, you know. In the gossip pages." Barbara puffed up a little and you could see her pride despite herself. "Angie was doing some kind of interview with him, I guess, for one of those papers she worked for, and she and him, they hit it off. He gave her a job, in his publicity department—but then, a few weeks ago, the whole relationship fell apart.

"It was the kind of thing that was always up with her. She'd get all excited and—"

"How long ago did they break it off?"

"Maybe a month. If that."

"And the last time you spoke with her?"

"Thursday before last. She was supposed to come over Sunday, like I said."

"She could be off on freelance assignment," said Nick Antonelli, but he was more tentative than certain. "That happens sometimes—all of a sudden."

"She always tells me," said Barbara.

"Maybe she just wanted to get away."

"She would call."

Dante thought again of his visit to the morgue, and wondered what to tell the Antonellis. Something must have passed over his face, because the pair of them regarded him with concern. Nick sat on the couch with his hands between his knees, dangling awkwardly. Barbara closed her eyes.

"This Michael Solano— Did you ever meet him?"

"No," said Barbara. "But Nick has."

Nick Antonelli shook his head.

"I don't really know him. It was business," he said. "You know, there's a shortage of commercial space right now. And his company— We were trying to see if we could work something out."

"What was your impression of him?"

Antonelli looked ill at ease. "Anything I would say," he said at last, "would not necessarily be based in anything. I mean he and Angie had some kind of relationship. She had gone to work for him, and I guess that's what prompted his people to call me. To look and see if we could provide his company with some space, make some kind of arrangement. But most of my dealings, they weren't with him. Not directly."

Dante talked to them for a little while longer, trying to get names of her associates, friends from work, but it became clear they did not know much about Angie's social life.

"So what's the next step?" asked Nick. "I mean, part of me, I understand, she's a grown woman, and she could have just gone off for a few days. You know something ends, and you go off, and you don't necessarily tell your parents."

Antonelli stopped then. He was trying to convince himself.

"It's not like her," said Barbara.

"So what's the next step?" repeated Nick.

Dante had been through this often as a cop. Though the guidelines had been firmer then, at least in theory, there were always judgment calls. When to tell the loved ones. When to hold off. He had seen the body, true, he'd seen the list of effects—but, in the end, to be definitive, you needed fingerprints, or dentition, or some scrap of DNA.

"A case like this, you usually work backward. Try to figure out the last time anybody saw the missing person. You talk to acquaintances, look at credit card receipts, phone records. I think . . ." He hesitated. "Her apartment— I would like to take a look around."

"I have a key," said Barbara. "I put out some food for her cat a few days ago. . . . He's very skittish."

"The cat is a head case," said Nick.

"He won't let anybody touch him but Angie. Angie was always like that, taking in strays."

"I've got something you should know," said Dante.

"What is it?"

"Your daughter . . ." His voice was flat, but he had to stop a second to keep it that way, without emotion: to keep his face empty like the face of a cop. In that instant he knew he had communicated more than he wanted, but he had no choice but to go on.

"Day before yesterday, Wednesday morning, the police pulled a woman from the bay, down on the Embarcadero."

Barbara and Nick Antonelli were fixed on him now and he recognized their expression from his time in Homicide. He was no longer the person they had come to for help. He was the messenger—an ambassador from the realm below, a shade in the guise of a familiar, appearing with news they didn't want to hear.

"What are you saying?"

"The body hasn't been identified. But I went to the morgue."

"Is it her?"

"The body had been in the water for a while . . . but the characteristics . . . the age . . ."

He handed her the list of effects.

"There's lots of women this size," Barbara said. "And the effects—a lot of women have clothes like this."

"That's true," he said. "They're searching the database for fingerprints . . . and we, if they can't get a match, we may want to get Angie's dental records."

"Do the police suspect foul play?"

"They don't have much to go on yet. The body was in the water maybe five days. Where the drowning happened exactly, whether it was at the pier, or somewhere else—it's hard to say. And . . . they're double-checking the blood analysis, to see if the alcohol content—"

Nick Antonelli responded angrily. "She's not the kind of person who would wander drunk down to the wharf and fall in the goddamn water. She is a goddamn beautiful young woman. Responsible. Mature."

Dante lowered his head.

"She's not dead," said Antonelli. At that moment, it was hard not to feel for this man. To remember him standing out there in the square, proud as hell, holding his young daughter by the fist. "I want you to find my daughter."

"I want to find her, too," said Dante. "It might be a good idea if I looked at her apartment. There might be something there to get me started."

Nick Antonelli leaned back in his chair. He wore a shirt that was tight across the chest and accentuated his biceps. He leaned over and took a taste of his drink and it made his face go ugly and strained, like he had just taken a sip of poison. Barbara did the same. All the glamour in her features had disappeared.

"I'll get the key," she said.

FIVE

Eccentric the Cat lay in an unhappy somnolence on his mistress's rayon bathrobe, in the dark corner of the armoire. It was a place that was redolent of Angie's smell, of her underarms and her fluids. Over the last ten days or so, Eccentric had been much traumatized. The night Angie had disappeared, some strangers had shown up and stayed into the small hours, nesting on the bed, moaning and rolling about. Eccentric had kept himself hidden that whole while, resentful of their smell, their intrusion. The people had left, but Angie had not returned, and eventually Eccentric had been forced to forage. He was walleyed, always misjudging his leaps, and the big tom that lived in the alley tormented him. Eccentric might have starved if Barbara Antonelli had not come by a couple of times to fill his bowl. Even so, the woman made him skittish, and the big tom was getting more bold. Last night the animal had even entered the apartment, coming through the cat door and sleeping in the armchair. So Eccentric had lain in the armoire, attuned to the intruder's every movement, to his wheezing breath and his ammoniac smell. In the morning, the tom had gotten into

Eccentric's litter box and scuffled sand all about the kitchen before leaving. Eccentric had scuttled deeper into the armoire. Now he heard the chatter of human voices in the hall, and the footfalls approaching, but they were not the right footfalls, the weight and preponderance of them were not correct—and he was at any rate still in his somnolent state, surrounded as he was by the closet smells, feverish with hunger, aching from his many falls and his battles with the tom. The key turned in the lock. Though Eccentric barely moved, he was instantly in a preternatural state of alertness and alarm. His hair raised in a high ruff. His claws tightened. His eyes widened. He was torn between hunger and his desire to burrow himself deeper in his mistress's clothes.

SIX

Barbara Antonelli fitted the key into the lock, but then Dante stopped her, touching her on the shoulder. She looked up at him. She resembled her daughter, but then she didn't. In the dark light of the hall she appeared younger. She had a distracted air. It was a look he'd seen on Angie, as if there were a nervous, trapped thing inside her, and the resemblance gave him a peculiar sensation. It was like one of those wooden dolls that came apart at the middle. Twist it open and there was another doll inside, identical but only smaller. Then another doll inside that.

"Let me go in first," he said.

"Why?"

"It's just a good idea."

"I've been in once already."

"It's just a good idea," he repeated. "I've done this a number of times—and . . ."

On the drive up, they had talked. Not about the case, but about Angie. About what she had been doing these last years. Some big articles, here and there. But the freelance work was uneven. Her father had helped out when she let him, but she didn't like taking his money. She had a love-hate thing with her dad. Always trying to impress him. He would've helped her buy a place, but she didn't want the help. So she had gone on living on Green Street, in her flat on the second floor.

"She likes it," Barbara had said. "The urban thing. And North Beach—it has an attraction for her. She's a sentimental girl."

Now Dante walked in ahead of Barbara Antonelli. It was just a precaution. He had walked in a lot of doors over the years, and sometimes there were surprises.

"Wait here," he said.

He gave the place a quick scan, taking in the details. The phone machine with its flashing lights, the mail stacked on the counter, the armoire with the silk nightgown draped over the top of the cabinet door.

It was a modest apartment, built shotgun style, with a bay window in the front and a kitchen at the back. The room in front could be divided by a pair of pocket doors. At the far end was a desk that looked out over the street—a wooden desk with a flower vase to one side and a bookshelf overhead. Her bed was draped with a gold duvet and there were a lot of pillows. The place was naturally dark, as were a lot of places in San Francisco, but she fought that with floor lamps and bright colors.

The place felt like her. Arranged but not arranged. A certain carelessness, not altogether unstudied.

Barbara Antonelli came in behind him now. It was apparent she was both ill at ease and glad to be here, taking comfort in her daughter's things and getting tearful at the same time.

Inside, the kitchen was scattered with litter.

"The litter was in its tray last time I was here. That cat . . ."

Barbara went out the back door onto the fire balcony and began calling for the cat. She had a low, sweet voice, and for a second Dante thought he heard something stir in the bedroom. When he looked, there was nothing.

Dante went to Angie's desk. It was an old-fashioned wooden desk with a single drawer underneath. Inside the drawer were paper clips and rubber bands and the usual office stuff. There were also some pictures that looked to have been taken on a boat, down south somewhere, off the California coast.

On the refrigerator, more pictures.

Angie with her dad, somewhere here in The Beach.

Her mom, alone.

The family house down the street, twenty years ago.

An award for journalistic excellence.

A picture of a young man, midthirties, with thick black hair. He had soft looks, a big smile, a certain confidence. There had been a picture of the same man, he and Angie together, in the photos in the desk drawer.

"Who's this?"

"That's him. Michael Solano."

"You haven't met him, though?"

"No—just pictures. Like I said, they were going great guns for a while, he and Angie. Then I don't know. Something happened."

"Was she depressed about it?"

"Not enough to throw herself in the water—if that's what you mean."

Dante regarded the picture of Solano, and though it didn't make any sense—though there hadn't been anything between himself and Angie for a long time—he couldn't help regarding Solano as if the man had stolen something from him. Dante felt a curl of resentment, of jealousy even, and for a moment he understood the looks Nick Antonelli used to give him.

"I called Solano's office. After Angie went missing."

"What did he say?"

"He was surprised to hear from me at first. I think he thought I called to scold him. About the breakup."

"Did you?"

"I only wanted to know if he'd seen Angie."

"Had he?"

"Not for a while. After they broke up, she quit her job—and he hadn't seen her since. So I came down here. I looked around, and I saw Angie's suitcases were still here. And the mailbox was full, like I said. So I brought the mail inside. And I cleaned up a little."

"How much cleaning did you do?"

"Just a wine bottle—and some plates. And"—she looked confused for a second—"some foil wrappings. That cat, I guess he got into the trash . . . And I made the bed."

Her face was red now, embarrassed. It was her proper side, he saw. The nervous part that couldn't stand things out of order. That kept things in place.

"This nightgown . . . It needs to be laundered."

"Leave it," he said. It was the cop in him, the years of homicide. "We don't want to move things too much."

But she'd already taken the gown down by then. She stood there stiffly. "I'll just fold it up. I'll just put it away."

In many ways, he would have done better to inspect the apartment alone. He would have had an easier time of it. But Barbara had wanted to come. Had insisted. If nothing else, the cat needed food in his bowl.

"What kind of computer did she use?"

"I don't know. One of those laptops."

"Do you know where it might be?"

Barbara was at the window now. He feared she might be about to fall apart on him. When she turned, though, she was composed. Forcibly, perhaps—but still composed.

"On her desk?"

"No," said Dante. "It isn't there."

Dante went to the phone machine. The display said there were a half dozen new messages on the phone. He pushed the button and ran through them. An after-hours telemarketer. Her hairdresser, reminding her about an upcoming appointment. The dry cleaner's.

Then . . .

Hey, Angie, this is Jim Rose. I'm back in town, and I was wondering if you still wanted to get together later today. We could meet—

Just then, Angie had cut in.

"Jim," she said.

The recording had cut off the instant she spoke, and now the room was quiet. Dante remembered how such moments—on an investigation, when you heard the voice of the missing—used to give him a chill.

"That was her," said Barbara. Her face was flush. "She talked to that man on the phone. She picked up."

"Yes."

"So, maybe—"

"It was last week," he said.

Dante ran through the rest of the messages, listening to the times, the days. The hairdresser again. More missed appointments. The man Jim Rose, it seemed, was the last phone call Angie had taken before she vanished.

"Who is this Jim Rose?"

"I don't have any idea."

If this were a police examination, and the cops suspected foul play—if they got serious—the police would tear the place apart. Look through the bookbindings, behind the cupboards, under the loose floorboards. Sift through the dirty clothes, her trinkets, and her juvenilia. But in a case like this—Missing Persons—it could take a while for the cops to get moving, and they might not even come at all. The advantage, from Dante's point of view: The place wasn't a crime scene, not yet, and for the time being it was within his purview to take it apart if he wanted.

Barbara stood by the bureau. She had opened the jewelry box and was fishing through for something.

"Angie's pearls," she said. "A string her father gave her years ago."

"Are they there?"

She shook her head. Dante said nothing, but he knew what she was getting at. He knew the implication. There had been pearls on the death manifest, among the articles of the deceased.

She shut the box, opened a drawer. Shut that, too.

"Angie had a way of scattering things."

"I know," he said.

"I appreciate your doing this. I realize, it must be hard on you, too."

"I'm glad to help."

There was the silence between them—and then he heard something stir again. Over there, he thought, behind the wall.

"What happened between you and Angie?" Barbara asked. "Back then?" It was a funny time to ask, some ways, but such moments were when things like this came out, he knew; when people said the things they otherwise didn't say. "I have often wondered. I mean, you two, you seemed very close, and I thought . . ."

"We were fond of each other."

"So what happened?" she said, and there was note of accusation there, and hurt—as if, she thought, somehow, their breakup was a reflection on her.

"We were young."

"You loved her?"

Dante met her gaze.

"Who couldn't love Angie?"

He could tell she wanted something more. He didn't know what to say. He went over to the refrigerator and looked at the calendar. The Sunday before last had been circled, dinner at her mother's, and this coming Tuesday:

The Utah Hotel. 7 p.m.

"That list of effects," she said. "Those pearls . . . and Angie had a new skirt, you know—from Dazio's. I'm going to see if it's in the armoire."

Dante wanted to stop her, to prevent her from disturbing the lay of things, but she was moving too quickly. In that same instant, he heard the stirring again, then a sudden wail that ascended in volume as Barbara swung open the cabinet door.

The cat came flying out—a white blur that bounced wildly against the cabinet door and shot into the room.

Barbara shrieked.

The animal bolted across the bed, hit the wall next to Dante, then scurried hard across the hardwood, scampering and howling, bounding madly toward the tiny flap in the kitchen door.

It took the better part of an hour, plus the help of the man in the flat upstairs, to lure Eccentric out of his hiding place and into the carrier. Barbara Antonelli had decided she could not leave the animal at the apartment untended, but the cat shied from her and would not come when she called. Eccentric did not much care for the carrier. He howled and sputtered and moaned, then kept up the noise even as Dante drove through the darkened streets of The Beach. The racket continued until they were within a couple of miles of Antonelli's place in San Mateo, then abruptly stopped—as if the animal had suddenly died, or suffered a seizure.

Dante was grateful.

Up ahead, the house was dark. Nick's car was not in the driveway.

"Do you want me to wait with you until he gets back?"

Barbara Antonelli shook her head.

Dante looked out at the front yard. Fruit trees. Stone miniatures. A piece of driftwood in the shape of a snake. The wind was coming down the canyon and he could smell the eucalyptus and hear the oleander rustling in the breeze.

"Nick," she said. "He hasn't changed."

Dante nodded.

She reached out and touched his hand. There was something unspoken. The family pearls. The designer skirt. Nick's philandering. But there was something else, too. Something she was not saying. She took the carrier and disappeared into the darkened house.

On his way up the peninsula, Dante kept his eye on the rearview.

Part of him wondered if he should have left Barbara Antonelli alone. He guessed she would be all right. She was a strong woman. And the neighborhood was safe.

Dante lived in a walk-up over Columbus Avenue. Once upon a time, it had been Longinus Drugs below, and the upper stories had been inhabited mostly by Calabrians, every one from the same village back in Italy. For a while, according to local rumor, the poet Corso had lived here, and was visited by his famous East Coast friends, writers who stopped off during their cross-country drives to hang their heads from the window and vomit into the dago streets.

Poems about madmen. About angels who whispered in your dreams. About the the end of time and the light that contains within it the memories of the dead.

Dante didn't give a shit about poetry.

In some ways the building had not changed much. The plumbing had gotten older, and the window casements had swollen, but the inhabitants were still mostly immigrants, Chinese families for the most part, trying to get a foothold. But there were transients and cripples as well, same as the old days. Single men. Alcoholics. Also, a couple of hardcore punksters, pale skin and Day-Glo hair, eyes zippered shut, playing like they were Syd and Nancy down the hall.

Dante checked his phone messages.

Nothing from Marilyn. There was, however, a call from Tom and Lisa, his tenants on Fresno Street, complaining about a noise in the attic.

Their rent was due. And it was the second time they'd called. He'd go out there tomorrow, he told himself. He'd climb up the ladder into the attic and see what was going on. His guess, there was something nesting in the rafters.

In the meantime, he should call Marilyn.

They were on the skids. His fault. He and Marilyn had been making plans, not too different from those in the rumors—but in the end Dante was not really so sure he had been ready to let his father's place go. But he hadn't wanted to live there either.

So when Lisa and Tom had appeared, going door to door, trying to find a place to live, any place, he had rented them his father's house, down there on Fresno.

Marilyn was furious.

The city was packed, rents were tight, and he had let it go for half of what he should. Even so, that was not the real reason for her anger.

He should go to Marilyn, he knew. He should not wait too much longer. He changed his clothes and went outside. The dinner hour was over and the couples were on the street, a little drunk, a little giddy. Dante lingered out front, hands deep in his pockets, just lingering. With his long nose and his white shirt and his black pants. Looking like some guy on a street corner, some guy from the old days, just hanging out, hands in his pocket, waiting for his buddies to show. He glanced up the hill toward Marilyn's. He imagined her bright apartment. He imagined the smell of her as she opened the door and her big laugh and her dark hair. When he reached the square, he went the other way, down through Mortuary Row, up Green Street.

He climbed Angie's stairs. He checked her armoire. He checked the little jewelry box. But that which he feared was true. There was no Dazio skirt. There were no pearls. They were on the manifest, but they were not in her room.

SEVEN

Jake Cicero had the vague feeling his life was coming apart on him. He had no reason to expect so, but Cicero had experience in such matters, both as observer and participant, and had learned over the years to trust his intuitions.

"Oh, Jake," he said to himself. "You've got to relax."

Cicero told everyone he was sixty-two years old, but he was in reality seven years older than he claimed, and for this reason many of his acquaintances thought he looked like hell for his age. He had heart palpitations sometimes, but the problem was not his age, Jake told himself. The problem was he did not get enough sleep. Precious sleep. Sweet sleep. He'd been running Cicero Investigations since 1959. Over forty years now—and never enough sleep. He had started out with divorce cases, but for the last twenty years his bread and butter had been contract work for the city: investigating for the public defender's office. But it wasn't all city business. There were other cases. Affairs to investigate, sure. Business partners to pursue. Or missing persons, like Angie Antonelli, who vanished without explanation.

These days he had three investigators out in the field, plus a clerk for the office, but it seemed harder than ever to find the time he needed to just close his eyes.

Fuck it, Jake, he told himself, and he swung his feet up onto the desk.

He leaned back and felt himself drifting. All he needed was a little taste of dreamland, a sweet moment. Some day I'll just die here, he thought, and he almost smiled at the thought. A wry smile. Someday I'll just snooze right out with the phone ringing and never come back. Same as my father did—in his law office, right about my age, dreaming of some place he'd never been, maybe, a face he could not quite remember . . .

Cicero's phone rang.

It was his wife, Louise. She was his third wife—his fourth, really, if you counted those two lost weeks he'd spent with a beautiful schizophrenic in Reno. But that had been annulled and not too much later he'd married Louise. Louise Goode. Not yet divorced when they'd met, the estranged wife of one of his clients. She was twenty-odd years younger than himself and had a demure manner, just graying elegance, pale skin, and a softness that belied something cold underneath. Just turned forty-five the day they'd met. That is, if she were telling the truth. It didn't matter. There was something about Louise he couldn't resist. A steeliness in her sensuality. A hunger. They'd been married two years.

"Jake," she said now, over the phone—and the way she said it made him think of how she looked in bed, hovering over him. The way her mouth opened and you could see her teeth. "I've got the brochures."

He felt something flutter inside. Louise had been talking lately about a cruise. It was something that had started down at the racquet club. Jake didn't care for the club himself, but she looked good in those pleated skirts, out on the court.

"I thought we had till the end of the month to decide about that."

"We do, but accommodations—those are first come, first served. It would be nice to have a suite with a balcony."

"Let's talk about this tonight," he said.

"I really don't want to go by myself, honey. I really want you to come."

He'd been on a cruise ship years ago, and he wasn't crazy about it. Ports of call and duty-free liquor and overpriced artwork and long hours at dinner tables with strangers and not a fucking thing to say. It was no Orient Express.

"You're too young for a cruise. Why do you want to waste yourself on a boat full of old men?"

"Don't be silly," she said. "You're not so old."

Something about the way she said it put a knife through him. Earlier, he'd suggested she go on her own. That he wouldn't mind. He had his business here to take care of. The truth was, though, he didn't want her to go without him.

"Anyway, I just wanted to know when you would be home."

"Around seven."

"All right," she said. "I'll be here, waiting."

The last time Louise had said that, though, she hadn't been home. She'd been out with her girlfriends at the club. And Frank Strum, the attorney.

"Oh Jake," he whispered to himself again.

He should turn his attention to his work, but he was thinking about Louise. He and she were alike in more ways than one. They'd both been married several times, and they both had lives they'd left behind. People they'd abandoned. Louise had resisted him at first, he remembered, same as his first wife.

Jake thought of them sometimes, his various wives. Alice, his first, and their seven years together. Then Jeanine, with her blond hair and her blousy looks, who'd ultimately grown to regard him as a fool. And from those two marriages, three kids—none of whom regarded him as their father.

Sometimes he wished he could go back in time and set all that straight.

There was a knock on the door.

Dante Mancuso entered. He was a sticky one, Mancuso. Cicero had known Dante when he was a young homicide cop. At the moment, Dante stood in the doorway with his fists all but clenched. He had penetrating eyes and an old-fashioned nose—the kind of nose you didn't see much anymore, a fisherman's nose, a big hook to drag in the sea. Dante smiled, somewhat thinly. Cicero had known Dante's mother, too, and the smile reminded him of her. A beautiful woman, before she'd gone to the asylum.

"Oh, the man of the hour," said Cicero.

"Why do you say that?"

It was one of his stock phrases. Cicero had no idea why he said such things. Because it was what his own father used to say to him, maybe, when young Jake had found his way back to the house from some errand. Or for no reason at all. Because it didn't make any difference, as soon as you walked into the door, whoever you were, you were the man of the hour, because you were the person who was there. Here. Now. You were the one who existed. Who stood in this room. Whose heart was beating.

"The Antonelli case," Cicero said. "I was just thinking about that. The father called twice this morning. He wants to know what you've got."

"I shouldn't have told them about the body."

"Maybe not. But they'd be twisting either way. Meanwhile, Antonelli's been hounding the cops, too. You know what kind of guy he is. Has to have everything. Have it now."

"I know."

"So what have you found out?"

Dante caught him up. He'd been working all morning to track down the man on the phone machine, Jim Rose. So far, he didn't have much. Rose didn't have an address in the city, at least not one they could find.

"According to the phone company, he called from his cell phone—one of those cash specials bought down at Radio Shack, a store down in the Castro. But no address on the application."

"But he called from within the city?"

"That's what the records indicate. And one of Angie's last credit card purchases, it was at Dazio's. A silk skirt. Beige."

"Any significance?"

"The corpse was wearing one like it. It's on the manifest. And so are the family pearls."

Jake Cicero lowered his head. Himself, he wasn't wild about Nick Antonelli. The guy had had him investigate some of his business clients once upon a time, looking for dirt, and he'd put a fidelity tail on his own wife, though by any rights it should have been the other way around. Also, Cicero knew the stories about how Antonelli's father had rough-handed things to get his way along the waterfront, and how Nick himself had maintained his father's connections.

To Chicago. To old man La Rocca.

Truth was, La Rocca had died, and the son had moved to Vegas, and the talk probably was just talk, jealousy, people running down anyone who did well. Antonelli did nothing to discourage it. The way he blustered, it was tempting at times to wish the man ill. Even so, Cicero didn't want to be the one to tell him about his daughter. It would be hard to take any pleasure in that.

"Was the body good for prints?"

"Yes."

"So—what's keeping those sons of bitches? All they gotta do is throw the prints into the system. See if they match."

"You know how it is. Missing Persons. They're not in a rush."

"Maybe the body . . . the prints . . . ," Cicero hesitated. "Maybe it's not her." He shrugged. It was always possible, after all, that there would be no match.

Dante said nothing.

"How about her boyfriend, what's his name, Solano? You talked to him yet?"

"I have an appointment this afternoon. He's been in L.A. the last few days. New York before that—drumming up venture capital."

Cicero nodded.

"Maybe you should go back to her apartment, see if you can find something else. Once the cops move on this—if they move on it—your access might be limited."

"All right."

"I got a retainer from Antonelli. It's a good retainer. So . . . well . . ."

"So you want me to burn some hours."

"That's not what I meant."

Mancuso was an edgy one, Cicero knew. Capable, but a bit of a wild card. He'd been an up-and-comer with the SFPD, a young cop with a chip on his shoulder. Too stubborn for his own good, and so he'd taken a fall. He'd left the force and gone to work down in New Orleans. Private industry, Dante claimed, but Cicero had tracked it down and he knew better. It was a government front, some kind of agency work. Rumor was, Dante had walked over the line in the way that happens in such work. He'd developed habits, dependencies. A taste for the street-corner wares that the agency had used at one time to finance its backdoor operations. Dante himself seemed clean now. Or clean enough. Anyway, Cicero had hired worse. Mancuso was a good investigator, and the Antonellis had requested him. Because Dante had been close to their daughter. Because their families had known one another and there'd been a romance of some sort back when Dante and Angie were kids.

"How well did you know the girl anyway?"

"Pretty well," said Dante.

Cicero waited for more but it didn't come. Himself, he had seen the Antonelli girl, three, maybe four times, when her family still lived in The Beach. He had a memory of her—twelve years old, or thereabouts, on the cusp of bigger things, skinny legs and big brown eyes, restless in Washington Square with her mom and dad, but that could have been any mom and dad strolling with their just-blossoming kid in the park on a North Beach Sunday.

"I'll talk to the boyfriend this afternoon," said Dante.

"All right," said Cicero. "Let me know how it goes."

Dante left, and Cicero put his feet back onto the desk. He closed his eyes. It was a morose business, his line of work. Maybe he should go on the cruise after all. It might be a pleasant thing. He could lean back in a deck chair with the sea breeze in his face. He could listen to the ocean, to the rattle of the ship and the clinking glasses at the bar, and not worry about conversations like the one he'd just had. Missing persons. Infidelities. Business deals gone rotten. Whatever it was people whispered about, he need not pay attention. He need not listen. It would all be someone else's concern, details lost in the churning of the wake, in the cawing gulls, in the sound of the hot tub and the not-so-young honeymooners playing Ping-Pong on the deck. He could get some sleep. Even now, thinking about it, he began to nod off. He heard the foghorn out in the bay and smelled the sea air through the window. That was the thing about North Beach. It might not be a port town anymore, but the memory of what had once been mingled with the present. As he got older, this kind of thing seemed to happen more often. The brain got soft, and in his dreams the living mingled with the dead. People said this was a sign of deterioration, but maybe it was the opposite. Maybe he was moving toward something. Some reconciliation.

He remembered a time some forty years ago, a Christmas Day in the little house down in San Bruno, his first wife and himself and his son around a brick fireplace, an image like something from a Polaroid, and all of the sudden now he gasped, like his father had, maybe—short of breath, a palpitation in his chest—a gasping set off, though he didn't realize it at first, by the ringing of the phone.

It was Nick Antonelli. Again.

"I just talked to the police," said Antonelli, and Cicero knew what was coming. He could hear it in the man's voice. "My daughter . . ."

"I know," said Cicero. "I'm sorry."

"What do you mean, you know? What do you fucking know?"

"What did the police say?"

"If you knew, why didn't you tell me? I am not paying you to learn things from the police."

"We had our fears . . . but the police, the final determination . . . We couldn't say more until the identification was definitive."

"Yeah, well, fuck you."

Cicero let it pass. The man was in the throes of grief, and people said funny things. Except, in Cicero's opinion, Antonelli had always been somewhat of an asshole.

"They want me to take the body. This is the first thing the cops say, I have to make arrangements. But how can I do that? These bastard police—they're not interested in what really happened."

"They wouldn't release her if they hadn't completed the lab analysis. If there's some other tests you want to run, in case of a criminal trial—"

"No one's rushing me. I am not burying her until I goddamn know what happened."

Cicero knew better than to argue. He'd had a client who kept her son's body in cold storage for two years in the event a killer was found, and the body held additional evidence. Truth was, it wasn't necessary. The coroner's examination, his record, that was the forensic evidence.

But sometimes people just did not want to bury their dead.

"Dante's investigating," said Cicero.

"I want a chronology. Every minute. She didn't just fall into the bay."

"He's out there this minute. He's following the trail."

"Fuck you," said Antonelli.

Elegant, Cicero thought. Elegant fucking Italians. Dignified in death as in life. Masters of the oratorical phrase.

EIGHT

A half hour earlier, Nick Antonelli had been at his kitchen table, watching his wife. At that point, Antonelli had not yet talked to the police. At that point, he had not known, not for certain, that his daughter was dead. At that point, Barbara had been in the backyard, trying to retrieve the cat.

The cat did not respond to her. Eccentric had spent the night before underneath the furniture, then bolted outside when she'd opened the slider. Now the cat had gotten itself on the diving board, and his wife stood at the edge of the pool, trying to coax him back. Instead the foolish creature crouched, and looked as if it were going to jump across the pool—a foolish thing to do in any event, but more foolish given what Nick had seen of its leaping abilities.

Go ahead and jump, Nick thought. Go ahead.

Then the kitchen phone went off.

His wife turned toward him, watching. She wore a sleeveless dress, arms akimbo. Even after he turned away, phone in hand, he knew she was watching his every move, reading his posture. She didn't come in right away, though. She waited till the conversation was over.

"The police?" she asked.

"Yes. They found Angie."

Barbara went past him and sat on the sofa—in the big room with its straw mat wallpaper and the black piano and the imported ceramics. Her dress was olive green, the color she always wore. She sat with her head bowed and her shoulders straight. Outside, on the patio, on the other side of the glass door, the cat slunk into the bushes, disappearing into a velvet area of moss and ferns.

"She's dead then," she said.

Nick walked away from her, back to the bedroom. There was a sliding door here, too, looking into the backyard. European style, the real estate agent had said, back when they bought the place. Courtyard living. A statue outside and a fountain. Just like the goddamn Romans.

He'd torn it all out and put in a swimming pool.

On the bureau was a family portrait, the three of them together—something his wife had arranged a few Christmases back. He'd never liked the picture. It was too formal, and he looked silliest of them all.

And now his cell went off in his pocket.

It was a new addition, the cell, something he had gotten on the insistence of Anne Marie, his secretary. He did not much care for it. The device gave him trouble, and he was tempted for a moment to smash it against the wall.

On the other end was Mark Smith, down in Los Angeles.

Smith the Invisible.

Smith was Solano's financial officer, but Antonelli had never met him. Solano was the CEO, but it was Smith the Invisible who controlled everything. Smith the Unknowable. Solano was the company's public face, but the venture firm funding the operation had brought in Smith to watch the books. When the company needed office space, it was Smith who'd made the deal. It was a complicated transaction, but the essence of it was that Antonelli would use his holdings as collateral to buy the old Waterhouse Building, down in China Basin, then lease it back to Solano's firm. No sooner had the ink dried, though, than Antonelli had gotten word that Solano's funding was in jeopardy. Some insiders were causing trouble. It had been straightened out relatively quickly, though. Because of me, Antonelli thought. Because of my willingness to draw the line, to get tough. To make the calls that had to be made. But none of that mattered now.

"My daughter's dead," Antonelli said.

There was quiet.

"I'm sorry," said Smith.

"I'm going to find out what happened." The grief was apparent in Antonelli's voice. "I'm going to goddamn find out."

He heard his wife out in the yard. Barbara was calling the cat. Nick could see her through the windows, crouched over, peering into the bushes where the cat had disappeared. Her voice was high and sonorous, but the sight of her, piteous, full of grief, calling that goddamn cat, filled him with rage. "Goddamn cat."

"Excuse me?"

"Angie's cat—my wife lets it in, lets it out. That's all we have left of my daughter now. That goddamn cat."

The words came out peculiar. Like he cared about the cat. Like it meant something to him.

"My daughter's cat," he said.

"I see."

"I'm going to find out what happened to Angie. I told you a

couple of days ago. I've hired a detective, and I'll hire another. I'm going to find out what happened."

"These things . . . ," Smith spoke softly, with a certain coolness, a certain edge, like a man speaking from the ether. "Sometimes, maybe it's better to let these things go."

"What did you say?" Antonelli shot back.

There was no reply.

Despite himself, Antonelli felt a little jolt of fear. Outside, the cat skittered out of the bushes, back toward the diving board. Nick felt again the dread that had been palpable in his chest since Angie disappeared.

"What did you say?" Antonelli repeated.

He never had liked these son of a bitches: the dot-com people with their smugness. They had this demeanor, this attitude—all the rules had changed and you couldn't possibly know, couldn't possibly understand. You should just be glad they talked to you. Count yourself blessed. He had structured the deal cleverly, dealing from his gut, but there'd been a rush to it, the way these new people rushed everything, and he wondered now, old bull that he was, if he'd charged too soon.

"I'm sorry for your loss," said Smith.

"Sure," said Antonelli.

Whatever Smith's original reason for calling, he didn't reveal it now. He let Nick go. Nick looked down at the family portrait. He batted it to the floor. Then he batted himself against the blue bedroom wall, wailing—and at length exhausted himself on the carpet. And when he was done, he lay with the picture in his hand. His poor daughter. Happy, smiling, full of vulnerability. That bastard Mancuso should have married her, he thought. Him and his ugly fucking nose.

"Son of a bitch," he said.

And then he rolled over on the floor. He wailed. A week ago he had had the world in his hands, but now . . .

He walked over to the bedroom phone and called Cicero again, demanding action. When the conversation ended, he took the receiver and broke it against the wall.

A couple of hours later the doorbell rang. Barbara was on the kitchen phone, speaking in that low, tender voice of hers, almost sensuous. Someone had called a few minutes before on the house line, but it had been for her apparently, not Nick. Something about his wife's posture made him pause, but then the doorbell rang once more.

A young woman stood in the entry, clipboard in hand. She was a rangy girl who wore her hair in a fall.

She was looking for donations, for some clinic in the city. You didn't get much of that up this way, and it made him wonder. When she smiled at him, though, he could not help it; despite everything, he smiled back.

At the same time, though, he could hear Barbara. Something about arrangements. Something about papers that needed to be signed. Then he realized she was talking to Gucci's kid, lousy-ass mortician down at the Diamond Mortuary. *No, before anything like that, before they put Angie in the ground . . .*

Nick walked away from the young woman at the door.

"No," he said to Barbara. "Tell Gucci no. Before we sign a release, we're going to Columbus Station. We're making sure the cops do their goddamn job."

Barbara put her hand over the receiver.

"We have an appointment at the mortuary," she said.

"To hell," he said.

He stomped away. Outside, in the backyard, the cat was back on the diving board, eating some food Barbara had set out. Then the fool beast curled itself out on the edge, over the water, as if it were the most natural place for a cat to be.

NINE

Solano Enterprises was in the Jackson Cannery, down in the flats below Telegraph Hill. There had once been a beach here beneath the cliff face, and a shallow inlet, but that inlet had been backfilled long ago. The cannery had been built sometime in the twenties, and it stood against the sheerness of the cliff, a red brick building where the Calabrian women had worked the lines once upon a time, in their black dresses and their hairnets, sorting and stewing and packing. A different kind of work went on in the building now, though the nature of the produce was a bit harder to determine.

Solano's company had two floors, in the far wing, but Solano himself was a somewhat vaporous presence.

Like a number of young men who headed up the small companies that had suddenly taken up residence beneath the Pyramid, he was often referred to as a visionary. But like a lot of these new visionaries, Solano could be hard to locate. He had many responsibilities, many places to be.

He was in Los Angeles for the day, his secretary said.

No, no, plans had changed. He was meeting with the technology team in San Jose. He was teleconferencing with Japan. On his cell to New York. In his car. In the conference room with the designers. He would be back this afternoon. Perhaps. Down the hall. In his dusk-gray rayon shirt. Smiling. His presence rippling the air.

Everywhere at once. Nowhere.

The rainmaker. The magnet. The one who brought it all together.

Solano had a number of gurus on his advisory staff. These included a businessman who wrote self-help books. A television producer. A stock market analyst. A political consultant who worked for Senator Feinstein.

These people were his brain trust. Their pictures were on the company Web site—with sayings, aphorisms, quotations from their columns and their books. For a fee, their collective wisdom would be streamed over the broadband network and delivered via proprietary software to the desktops of employees whose companies were insightful enough to connect to their services.

But, likewise, their presence was elsewhere.

Not here exactly. But not there.

Certainly not in the building.

There were people in the building, though. More and more these last months. Too many, in fact, for the small quarters in the cannery's old wing. Information designers and video techs, artists and computer programmers, personnel and marketing people. The employees had meetings, and if at times the meetings were vague—if at times it was not clear the exact nature of their enterprise—if the proprietary software system did not launch and the technology staff backpeddled—if their pay was low and they could not afford to participate in the general hilarity of the streets at the night—if at times they grew skeptical and sardonic and suspicious—they still had their stock options. Not worth anything yet, but they would be, you could count on it. When the company went public, all their work, all their patience, would at last pay off.

Michael Solano at the moment was in his office. He had not been there long, and there was someplace else he had to be in another minute. Meanwhile, he had a million messages on his cell, a million more on his e-mail. He had too many places to be, and for a second he felt as if everything were getting away from him. In many ways, it wasn't his company any more. He was working for the venture people now. For Smith. Smith himself was a cipher, a voice over the wire. This was the way of things, Solano knew. The virtual world. Still, there were times Michael Solano felt as if he himself were not real. As if the world itself, and everything in it, himself included, were being atomized, turned into light. But this was the direction of things, as he himself knew. You had to keep the faith. Still, there were times he wished it was like the old days, before the virtual world. When the bosses were big men, fat and corporeal, who sweated as they pleased and jacked off over their money.

A young woman entered the room.

She was dressed in black and had startling white hair but also a face full of freckles. She was young. Very young. She was new to the job, but Solano saw in her face the little thrill that people in the company seemed to feel when they ran across him. They wanted to possess him, to capture the moment and put it in a bottle.

It was what everyone wanted these days.

"Mr. Solano. There is a man here to see you."

"I was about to leave," he said.

But he was already too late. The man had entered behind her, and Solano could tell at a glance the visitor wasn't going to go away easily. He felt a spike of fear. Flesh and blood pinned to the moment, like a fish on hook. The man standing in front of him was an unusual-looking man, a face like some prehistoric bird, with dark, searching eyes—and the biggest nose Solano had ever seen.

Mr. Solano?"

"Yes."

"Dante Mancuso. I'm sorry, but I left a couple of messages earlier—"

"If this is a sales call— My secretary—"

"I'm afraid, no. That's not it at all."

Dante handed him his card.

"I'm working for Mr. and Mrs. Antonelli," he said.

Dante studied Solano for a reaction, but he couldn't read him. Solano was a good-looking man, the kind of man used to having people study his face. He had curly hair, eyes that took you in quickly. He knew how to smile, how to give you his attention. Still, there was a sense he didn't really see you, and there was also something clumsy about him, something unsure. That small hesitation, though, that flaw in the surface, was what drew people in, Dante guessed, the thing that made him likable. That, and his offhand charm. The fact you wanted to be seen by those eyes.

"A few days ago, Barbara Antonelli called you. To talk about her daughter."

"Have you found Angie?" Solano asked.

Dante nodded.

"Oh, good." Solano smiled.

Maybe it was just all those years in homicide, delivering bad news. Or maybe there was something about Solano he didn't like. Or maybe it was because Dante had just heard the morgue report from Cicero on his way here. Whatever the reason, Dante had the impulse to spit out the words and watch their impact. To deliver them in a way that was as nasty as the news itself.

"No," he said. "I'm afraid it's not so good."

"No?"

"The police pulled her body out of the bay a few days back."

If Dante had wanted to shake up Solano, maybe he had succeeded. The good looks disappeared, and an ugly quiver creased the man's face. Pain, Dante thought. Or something like pain. And maybe Dante took some odd pleasure in it. He watched Solano bury his head in his hands. The man held himself like that a little while, then reached below the desk. The gesture triggered something in Dante. He shifted onto the balls of his feet—but then realized Solano had one of those little office refrigerators beneath his desk. Solano fumbled and came out with a mineral water. He tried to open the bottle, failed, and went to the window, composing himself. There was a sense of theatre about it, maybe, but Dante could not be sure.

"Excuse me." Solano's voice trembled. "I'm sorry. Can I offer you something, a water . . ."

Dante shook his head.

Then Solano picked up the phone and told his secretary to have the design group start without him. His voice was more controlled now. Dante sensed the man's importance here in this world and he was envious, not for the power, he told himself, but because later Solano would walk down the hall and immerse himself in other business. He wouldn't have to go back and sift through Angie's room.

"I'm sorry if I was suspicious when you walked in. We have an open-door policy, and lately I've been getting a lot of unsolicited visitors. Sales, mostly. And when you showed me the card, the detective thing . . . I'm sorry. I've got juice in here, too . . . Crackers . . ."

"No, thanks."

Regarding Solano now, up front, in the flesh, Dante realized the thing he'd been looking for without admitting it to himself. It had nothing to do with the case, maybe, but Dante felt again that animal part of him that still regarded Angie as his own, even these years later. Dante wondered over the attraction.

Solano had a certain hardness, a certain glassy surface, but there was that other thing there, too. The sense you could give him a push and he would break apart on you.

Dante wanted to give him that push.

"Originally, her father hired us to see if we could find her," said Dante. "Now, I'm just trying to piece together the last few days of her life."

"If there's anything I can do . . ."

"When was the last time you saw her?"

"About three weeks ago. We were planning to go to Cabo together, but . . ."

"You didn't go?"

"I went." Solano stopped, drank some water. Thinking about Cabo San Lucas, maybe, and those hot sands in Baja. "I liked Angie, I liked her a lot—but she wanted something more. I mean, I got divorced a couple of years back . . . And I'm so involved here, with the company. I just wasn't ready."

"So."

"I broke it off, to be blunt. And she had a very hard time with it. She quit her job with us. I didn't mean for her to do that, but she got angry and stomped out."

"You didn't see her again?"

"She came to a meeting, that afternoon. She was professional . . . but that was it. And the next day, I went to Cabo alone."

Dante remembered how he and Angie had broken up. Or he remembered a street corner somewhere, the expression on her face. He didn't want to think about it.

"It's bit risky, isn't it, getting involved with an employee?"

"I shouldn't have, I suppose," Solano said. "But it was mutual, and well . . ." His eyes darted away, and Dante could see his confusion and something like remorse. "Listen, I want to be cooperative. Our company, though . . . We're going up for a new round of venture funding." Solano paused then, as if catching himself, but Dante had seen the cornered look and understood. This world was everything to Solano. If it came unhinged . . .

"I wish I could help more. It's just that after Cabo, I went to New York on business. I haven't seen her since."

"How long were you gone?"

"Until the twentieth."

Dante went through the dates in his head. By the time Solano returned from his trip, Angie had been in the water a couple of days. Solano had not been in town when she died.

"Angie worked in publicity?"

"We are not quite as formal with our titles here. The old business hierarchies, the old boundaries, some of that just doesn't apply anymore."

"The other employees, did they resent her—this woman, hired off the street, working with you so closely?"

"Maybe some people felt that way, but like I said, we aren't beholden to those kinds of boundaries. Besides, everybody in the company has stock options. We're all rooting for success."

The last time Dante had run into Angie had been some years ago, down at Carlo's bar, and she'd had that look newspaper people get: cocky and world-weary at the same time, with her innocence all smudged up. He guessed he could see how she would be attracted to this man. Angie liked being at the center of things. And Solano, with the twist in his smile, the pivot to the hips, slouching against his desk, here in this office . . .

Dante had with him the photos he'd taken from her apartment.

"I was wondering if you'd mind taking a look at these."

Dante showed him the photos one at a time. The first was of Solano himself.

"That was on her refrigerator."

"Oh?"

"When was the last time you were in her apartment?"

"I'm not sure. About a month ago."

He showed him another photo. Angie skittery in an electric blue dress, on the deck of a boat, with the California coast in the background.

"Where was this taken?"

"Catalina, I think. We were on a business trip, courting investors."

He handed him another.

"This man?"

"That's Bill Whitaker. He's our vice president of technology. He was there to provide a reality check. We have to make sure everything we do here, it's feasible. And the investors, they like to talk to him."

"And the empty place, there, who was sitting in that?"

"It's empty."

"Right—but I see the wineglass is full. And somebody must have taken that picture."

"You know, you're right. I am trying to remember . . ."

Dante handed him the last picture.

A thin-faced young man, with reddish hair, good-looking in a middle-of-the-country kind of way. He stood alone on the deck, with that same piece of California coastline behind him.

"Oh, yes. Jim Rose. Jim was also with us that evening. At the table. He took the pictures, I remember now."

"Jim Rose?"

The voice on the message machine.

"Yeah—he's an engineer. He was along, on the technical side."

"He works for you."

"He did."

"What happened?"

"Jim left the company."

"Why?"

"We get turnover, like every other business. The competition for talent is intense right now."

"Do you know where I could find him?"

"You could ask our personnel department. They may have a forwarding address."

"Angie and Jim Rose—they were friends?"

"At work he gave her the technical information for the press releases—and her job was to put a glow on it."

"How well did Rose know her? Did they socialize?"

"I don't know," said Solano. "I'm not sure." He looked at his watch. "I'm sorry, this meeting, they're waiting for me."

"Something else . . . Angie introduced you to her father?"

"Yes, I met him. Just once."

"You have a business relationship?"

"Not me, specifically, no. Listen, I'd be happy to talk about all this later . . . I don't know how clearly I'm thinking, I'm a little stunned . . . and the design group . . ."

Dante understood. The man didn't want to talk. But he knew also that Solano would be on the phone soon enough, consulting his public relations people, or his lawyers, or the venture people themselves, trying to figure out how to control the damage if the news got out about his affair, about the dead employee in the bay. Though Dante knew such maneuvering was inevitable, the kind of contingency planning a man like Solano had to consider, it nonetheless gnawed at him, and no doubt would have gnawed yet more if he had known how quickly Solano would be on his cell, dialing, doing just as Dante imagined. Solano's call, though, had to be patched. The connection was not immediate. As Solano waited for his call to go through, he could not help but think of Angie's death, and he felt a certain fear in his chest, a certain irreality, a sense of things veering out of control, of wheels within wheels, and in his fear he touched himself, looking for solidity, and Solano thought of the girl at the front desk, of all the people waiting to talk to him, and then he touched his cock, feeling winsome, thinking it was not half so big as the detective's nose.

TEN

Dante went down to the house on Fresno Street to see if he could determine the problem in the attic. Lisa had sounded blue on the phone, but a few months ago, when he'd let her and Tom rent the place, the couple had been happy enough. The pair had come out a year earlier from Philadelphia, but apartment space had been hard to find, and they'd been living for months in a motel in South City, down by the airport. So they had been pleased as hell with the house on Fresno Street, at least at first, loving everything about it, from the lath plaster to the ancient sink to the furniture Dante's father had left behind and the pictures still hanging on the wall.

Now Lisa opened the door. She was a dark-eyed young woman, friendly by nature. Usually she was pretty talkative, but today she was quiet, as if there were something on her mind. She followed Dante into the kitchen and stood with her arms crossed, standing sentry as he climbed the ladder.

Dante didn't get far. The attic hatch had been padlocked.

His father had put the lock up there, Dante remembered, because his mother had become obsessed with the attic. She had not been able to let things alone: pictures, old clothes, memorabilia. She'd unpacked, repacked, then unpacked again, all the time in conversation with people whose photographs lay strewn about the attic floor. Over time the conversations had become increasingly strange.

Now the lock was rusted, and anyway, Dante did not have the key. He could see the lock was not going to come off easily.

Toward the end, his mother had ripped up some of the photographs and burned others, but a number had survived. Among those was an uncropped copy of the communion photo. That day, it had not just been Dante and Angie standing on the steps in front of the church. In the original, there were other people behind them and to the side, some of whom his mother did not approve.

La Rocca and his Chicago friends.

Or so Dante's mother had said. But Nick Antonelli had been there, too, in the background, and relatives from both families and a number of other children, including a little boy off to the side, his face oddly blurred, out of focus, because the camera had caught him in motion.

Dante could not quite remember the boy, but something had happened, he knew, and the kid had left the school.

His mother had not liked these people in the background, so she had had them edited out. Dante, though, had been fascinated, and at some point he had spirited the original away, into his cigar tin. As far as he knew, that childhood tin was still on the other side of that padlocked hatch.

He climbed down the ladder.

"I'll have to come back," said Dante. "With bolt cutters."

Tom, Lisa's boyfriend, had wandered into the kitchen at some point and stood alongside Lisa, looking as if he had just woke up, unshaven, in his sweat pants and a T-shirt.

"At night, that's when I hear the noise," Tom said. "It sounds like someone's moving things around up there."

Dante nodded. There was loose planking beneath the soffits, and there were animals who made their living prowling the roofs. Also, he knew how the old house rattled and creaked, and how sound traveled in the alley.

"To be honest, I haven't heard much, not lately," said Lisa. Tom gave her a look as if to object—and Dante wondered what was up between them. "But I'm a hard sleeper—and Tom, he's up all hours. Researching stocks."

"Stocks?"

"Yes."

Lisa laughed. It was an awkward laugh, and for a while neither of them would meet his eyes. "About the rent," Lisa said all of a sudden. "We're going to be a couple of days late. We're waiting on a check . . . Tom's company had to let some people go."

"It's just a cash flow thing," Tom interrupted. "They're hiring me back next week. As a contractor."

Dante was surprised. Just a few weeks before, the couple had been all optimism. Tom's company was soaring, ready to go public. He'd had a key position, and Lisa was working at a start-up in the South Bay.

"It will only be a few days," Tom said. "Meantime, I've been day-trading. I have myself all hooked up in the den."

ELEVEN

Nick and Barbara had left the house, and Eccentric the cat did not at first hear the strangers in the yard. He lay on the edge of the diving board, lolling in the sun. He had been fed, there was more food in his bowl, and he lay languid as an old rag, eyes in a slit, watching the shadows dance over the blue water. He had heard the gate click, but it was just another sound in a world of sounds: insects and lawn sprinklers and vague rustlings in the bushes the other side of the fence. Now there were footsteps, and pretty soon a woman and a man stood at the edge of the pool with the sun behind them. They stood there like black slits, shadows painted against the light. "Hi, there, kitty." The woman laughed giddily. "Oh, hi, there. Kitty, kitty." Then she stepped up on the board. Eccentric froze. The young woman edged forward, still cooing, but with a touch of mockery, and the man laughed, too, and perhaps in that moment Eccentric recognized them, their voices, their smell. Perhaps he recognized them from that time when they had rolled on Angie's bed and he had lain hidden in the armoire.

Eccentric edged back, judging the leap, the distance over the blue water, but he was a clumsy cat, one paw already off the ledge behind him, another struggling to find purchase.

Meanwhile the woman kept coming, edging toward him, with that sound like a bird in her throat.

TWELVE

Later that evening, Dante headed toward Angie's apartment. Barbara Antonelli had given him the key, and he wanted to take another look without the mother around. On the way, he walked through Mortuary Row, as it was called—the little hollow below Columbus Avenue on the way up Russian Hill. It had been a meadow once, with a spring running through. Now the Diamond Mortuary crouched on the one side and the Green Street Mortuary on the other. Each institution had an awning over its doorway, and there was almost always someone lingering under those awnings. If not a mourner, than a shadow of a mourner. A footman, perhaps, or a limo driver, or some other functionary from the inner realm.

In the old days, the Northern Italians had frequented one side of the street, the Southerners the other, but both establishments were under the Chinese wing now—and at the moment there was no one under either awning. The doors stood open but vacant, and this vacantness was somehow more unsettling than any funeral entourages might have been.

Then, around the corner, suddenly appeared the Green Street

Mortuary Band: old men with their snare drums and their trombones and kazoos. They were a tradition in The Beach, these old men, in their lime green hats and marching jackets—wending their way through the streets on the behalf of the bereaved.

Oompah this, oompah that.

Stopping at the dead man's favorite bar. Slobbering in their tubas. Rat-a-tatting their drums and clicking their heels while the mourners followed behind and the tourists gawked. Dante remembered the old superstition: Cross the path of the parade before it had done passing, next time they will be marching for you.

This particular parade was at its end, the mourners dispersed, the band members returning. The marchers walked slowly, in no particular hurry.

Dante stood at the curb, letting them pass. He did not believe the superstition, he told himself, but abided nonetheless.

They had fallen silent now, the old men and women of the band—with their yellow-gray hair and rheumy eyes and skin like wrinkled buzzards. The only sounds were the shuffling of their shoes on the concrete and their heavy breathing and the vague tittering of the snare as it bounced against the belly of the drummer. It made a sound like a snake hissing.

They had all but passed. Dante started across.

Then he stopped in his tracks. In the back, bringing up the rear, was glass-eyed Elvis Marino. A man from the neighborhood. Old as hell. Half ghost himself. And with his good eye, he gave Dante a sudden wink.

Dante checked Angie's mailbox first, but there was nothing to speak of—some circulars, a lingerie catalogue with her name misspelled—and then he went up to her apartment. He trudged the stairs. He had resisted returning here, though in the end he knew he would come. The police were usually pretty slow to reclassify a missing person case, but if they did come—if they suspected homicide, or if Antonelli pushed hard for an investigation—then his access might soon disappear.

He went at it methodically this time, room by room.

The kitchen with its hanging utensils and its butcher block and the overstuffed drawer full of bank statements and bills. The living room with the desk in the bay window, the phone machine with its pulsing red light. The bedroom with its chest of drawers, its armoire, and its jewelry box.

He walked over and hit the phone machine, but the first new message was blank, and the second was a computer-dialed solicitation for a time-share in Hawaii.

He listened to the old messages again. He turned her bill drawer inside out. He went through her bureau, removed her panties and her sweaters. Searched under the bed and went into her pants pockets and her old purses and into her laundry.

He shook out the nightgown that Barbara Antonelli had folded, then he spread it on the bed, and searched the breast pocket, and examined the fabric for fluids.

There was a semen stain on the nightgown. A fresh stain, it seemed. He folded the nightgown and put it back on the chair.

Dante learned things from her receipts. She went on shopping splurges down in the Marina District. She bought shampoo and facial creams at a little shop down on Grant. She garaged her car down at Little City Garage. Her routine was mostly that of someone who stuck close to the neighborhood. Dry cleaner's. Hair stylist. Housecleaner every other Tuesday. Take home from the

Columbus Deli, down at the end of Mortuary Row.

The professional side of him knew most likely none of this would lead anywhere. Angie had fallen into the water and likely that was all anyone would ever know. If something else had happened—if she had been mugged, then pushed into the bay—then the answer to the crime wasn't likely to be in this room. Still, he took some comfort in being here. He took comfort in going through her things. But the truth was, you could go endlessly into the details of her life if you were not careful. You could follow every lead, walk every path, and still not know.

He glanced again at the nightgown.

But if her death were not an accident . . . If the killer was someone she knew . . .

He had leads to follow. The missing laptop. Jim Rose. The date circled on the calendar.

The Utah Hotel. 7 p.m.

From a circular in her desk he saw it was an industry event: a panel at which she was supposed to be in attendance. Also, Solano was supposed to be there, and Bill Whitaker, the lead engineer.

Dante went back to the armoire. It was here her presence seemed strongest to him. Her smell in the clothes, he guessed. Or maybe it was just the woman smell, the scent of perfume and dry-cleaning fluid and fabric tinted with exotic dyes, all these mingling with the musky scent of her sweat, of her stockings turned inside out on the floor, of her shoes, of her laundry still in the wicker basket.

He ran his fingers through her things. The straight skirts and working-girl jackets, the print blouses and bright scarves. Here were the everyday clothes, but also the things women bought and rarely wore. A ruffled shirt. An antique dress that might have been her grandmother's. A knee-length vicuña wrap.

What happened between you two anyway?

They had been young, like he'd told Barbara Antonelli. He had known Angie forever: her sand-colored hair and her freckles and her dark eyes haunted by that small window of light. Maybe they were just too close, maybe that was the reason. Maybe it was because he had not wanted Nick Antonelli for a father-in-law, or because once, a long time ago, when he'd been a little boy, Barbara Antonelli had put her fingers in his hair, and he had gone over and stood next to her daughter just to please the woman. Or because he could still hear his own mother's muttering in the attic and feel that darkness closing around him, and see Angie in that white dress on the church steps. Or because he had known Angie too long and too well, and in the end, when she wrapped her legs up around him and he put his tongue in her mouth and buried his head in the crook of her neck, he had been astonished at the feel of her, but at the same could not escape the feeling that he was somehow out on those steps again, with all those unseen people hovering and his mother still muttering *Save us, don't leave,* and Barbara Antonelli with that look in her eye like, at last, maybe, everything was going to be set right.

He glanced once more at the nightgown.

What did it prove? She'd been with somebody not long before she disappeared. A lab analysis might tell whom—but that kind of thing was best done by the police. The semen in itself, though, suggested nothing. She'd had sex. That's what people did.

But with whom? And when, exactly?

He had already gone through her armoire once, but now he went through it again, more slowly. He ran his fingers down one of her dresses. There was a looking glass on the door, and no doubt she had studied herself in its reflection, craning her neck over the shoulder the way women sometimes did, turning this way and that, trying to get a look at herself from every angle. He went on searching. He undid a blouse, examined a seam. He remembered her smell, the touch of her skin. Or almost remembered. He examined a skirt, navy blue. It had a long slit and high waist and he ran his fingers inside the waistband, where the material fit close to the stomach.

Nothing, he told himself. There was nothing here to go on.

Just cloth and fabric and scraps of paper. Some books on the shelves. A bed with an old comforter and the pillows thrown crookedly against the headboard. An odd collection of drinking glasses. A vase without a flower. A postcard from Spain, unsigned, from someone who had gotten infatuated with her in a bar some five years ago. A dining room table that had belonged to her mother. Silverware and a Giants cap and a silk scarf thrown over the top of the armoire door.

One of her dresses slipped from its hanger and fell to the floor. He tried to hang it back, but it slipped again and he laid the dress carefully on the bed.

She used to keep journals. When she was young, her journals had been a mix of words and pictures, sketches of birds and buildings. Of people from the neighborhood. Of her college campus.

Later, he knew, her journals had gotten detailed in a different way. She kept ideas for articles and also notes on things happening around her. He wondered if she had kept up the habit. If she did, he guessed, she had done so on her computer.

He lay down on the bed. Next to the dress.

I should not have left her, he thought. He closed his eyes and gritted his teeth and pushed the pillow under his middle and felt for the dress between his fingers. He listened to his heartbeat. He put his cheek against the dress. He opened his fist, and he closed it, and then he lay still.

In a little while he got up and hung the dress back where he'd found it. Barbara Antonelli had been embarrassed about the nightgown, he remembered. Embarrassed on account of the stain, he guessed—and because when she'd come to seek out her daughter, she'd found the bed unmade and the nightgown crumpled on the chair and a mess all around. She'd tidied things up, she'd told him. A wine bottle, she'd said. Foil scattered on the floor.

An idea came to Dante. An ugly idea. He pushed it away.

Dante wandered door-to-door, interviewing the other tenants in her building, but he learned nothing of any use. He sluiced his way down the dark hall and into the street. Mortuary Alley lay empty in front of him. He stopped then, out of intuition, maybe, or habit, scanning the alleyways, the door wells, the windows.

Nothing.

His job was to reconstruct her last hours. He stood on the corner, trying to put the sequence together, to imagine himself in her skin. She'd listened to the message on the machine upstairs; she'd changed her clothes and gone out. Maybe she'd paused here, where he was standing, then plunged down the hill, into the city.

Off to meet the mysterious Jim Rose.

Where that meeting had taken place, though, Dante had no idea.

He'd checked the phone records and the credit card stream, and the last charges on the card had been at the Columbus Deli, not long after Rose's call.

A pack of smokes.

After that there was no activity on the cards. No activity on her cell. Not a clue.

Dante imagined her walking down the street—in the Dazio skirt, the loose blouse, the pearls around her neck. He imagined her just ahead of him. Inside the deli, he showed her picture again. The grocer nodded, smiling, a bit lascivious, telling him yes, he had seen her, more than one occasion, but he could not say for sure when the last time had been. The men in the other pictures—Solano, Whitaker, Rose—no, they were not familiar. The grocer did not recognize them at all.

Dante stepped back onto Columbus Avenue.

Which way?

The streets cantered together from five directions. There were buses, taxis, streetcars. She could have gone any direction at all. Capps' Trattoria. Lin's Pedicure. Little City Parking. End of the World Café. Cavelli's Books. Some of these places had been around forever, but even if the names didn't change, the owners did. Still, the old ones were here. In the mortar. In the brickwork. In pictures packed in boxes. If he walked into Figone's Hardware with the photograph of Angela, and if the young clerk did not remember who she was—or if in fact the clerk did not know who Figone himself was, or the fact that Figone's son had sold this place to the hardware chain some twenty years ago, and both son and father were side by side now in Colma Cemetery—Dante would nonetheless smell Figone behind the counter, his wine breath and his cigars. Toward Broadway, the street grew crowded. Newcomers in their fresh suits, their khakis, and bright polos. Chinese teenagers. Tourists, underdressed for the evening chill. Up ahead, an old woman who looked like something out of another era, walking splay-footed down the street, veil over her head.

He had lost the trail.

Then he saw Marilyn Visconti. Marilyn, all burnished and sultry.

Old man Marinetti was with her, and Marinetti's daughter. They were ten feet ahead of him on the sidewalk. It seemed odd, surprising. But then he realized it shouldn't be. Prospero's office was right there. Marinetti was in his suit and tie, all dressed up, hair slicked down, and it occurred to Dante they were on the way to sign the papers that would put Marinetti's flat up for sale.

He paused, not wanting to overtake them on the street. Then they were gone, into the office. The crowd grew thicker, the street cluttered with traffic and noise. On he went. Into the business establishments, to show Angie's picture. Dante knew what was coming. The empty stares, the distressed expressions, the contradictory stories, gestures pointing this way, that, sending him out into the street, around the corner, down an alley, where her visage would appear momentarily, a shadow, a stranger who resembled her, the way the skirt moved, the turn of calf, the cut of her blouse, but then he would look again and she was gone.

THIRTEEN

Meanwhile, Daniel Gucci the funeral director sat with Barbara and Nick Antonelli in the comfort room of the Diamond Mortuary. Gucci was trying to make arrangements with the couple but not having an easy time. The Antonellis had talked to the police down at Columbus Station, he knew, and the police were ready to release the body, but in the course of that conversation Nick had grown belligerent. Or so he gathered. What exactly that problem had been, Gucci wasn't sure. Antonelli was a hothead, Gucci knew that. The undertaker had grown up in the neighborhood himself and seen his behavior plenty of times.

"I can't believe we're here," said Barbara Antonelli, and she looked at Gucci as if he were not quite real.

This was how it was. People in the neighborhood, even people Gucci had known all his life, viewed him as someone who did not quite exist—who lived in the shadows and only emerged at moments such as this.

Gucci asked if they had thought about the burial site.

"The family plot, where else?" said Antonelli. "Isn't that what my father paid your father for twenty years ago? Or have you put someone else in there?"

"No, no," said Gucci. "It's a beautiful site. Up there on the rise. I was just out there last week, when Cavelli's son . . . well . . . I only meant to say, there are several plots at your family site, and of these, which did you intend . . ."

He stumbled. The truth was, he'd never been comfortable in the business. He had inherited it from his father, then sold it to the Chinese. Now he was a kind of minor partner, dealing with the old Italian clients, the ones who'd left The Beach but still had ties here—those who attended the cathedral to take the sacraments, to get married, and to bury their dead.

"Earlier, we were discussing a vessel."

"A coffin, you mean," said Nick. "Well, this is the one."

Gucci hesitated.

"The Principessa, yes," he said at last. "Very beautiful."

Gucci knew the model. It was made from Italian oak, hand carved—inlaid with ivory and ornamented at the end with a hand-cast statuette of a young girl. It was quite elaborate, very expensive—and not in stock. Gucci could check the West Coast warehouse but chances were it had to be brought over from Italy. He tried to explain.

Barbara interrupted. "Angie said she wanted to be cremated."

Nick barked back. "Angie's not going to be goddamn cremated."

Gucci stared at his desktop. When he spoke again, it was in a stumbling voice that sounded rather like a man bursting into tears. It wasn't professional, but he could not help himself.

"I can order this for you. There might be a delay in the service—and there is also the issue meantime of storage. For the remains. And sometimes, it is better, for the sake of closure, to proceed a little more immediately. I have some very beautiful vessels, available more immediately."

"No," said Nick. "We will wait. I want this done right." Nick stood up then. He made a gesture as if dusting himself off. It was a gesture you saw the old Italians make as they got up from the table, dusting bread crumbs from their shirt. It didn't quite make sense in this context, but Nick made it anyway.

"Before you leave, the release form."

"What release?"

"So we can get her remains from the city."

"I'm not signing that."

"But—"

"I'm not signing."

Gucci said nothing. He had seen a lot over the years, and he knew how people could be. He cast his eyes toward Barbara Antonelli—a beautiful woman, he could not help but think, even now, in her grief, with old age around the corner—but she did not look back. She followed her husband out to the street, and Gucci felt himself becoming insubstantial again, a ghost behind the door, a figure from an old clock disappearing back into the mechanism.

Nick and Barbara were in their car now, heading home from the city. Nick was an aggressive driver, and his daughter's death had not slowed him down. He was stewing inside, blaming himself—then his wife. Because Angie was still living alone in that apartment at age thirty-two, unmarried. Because Angie had foolish ideas in her head that came from her mother's vague dissatisfaction with her life, from her mother's dissatisfaction with him. And it was that dissatisfaction, Nick told himself, that had made him act the way he did.

"I was going to give Angie this car," he said.

"I know," said Barbara.

"If she would take it. You know how she was. Try to give her something, and she says no."

They were in the BMW, the Series 7 Sedan: midnight blue with leather interior. It was true, he was about due for a new car. The sedan was going on three years old now—and he didn't care about the trade-in value. Except he knew how Angie was. He had tried to give her his Series 5 a few years back, but she'd said no. Like she was too good for the damn thing. When the truth was, she had a low opinion of herself. Didn't want to be seen driving around in anything nice. Better to give her father a little slap in the face.

"The police haven't finished their investigation. I don't see how they can put her in the ground until they've finished their investigation."

"Angie wanted to be cremated," Barbara said again.

"Angie said lots of jackass things. All I know—the police in Europe keep the body until there's a trial. They don't put the goddamn evidence in the ground."

Barbara didn't say anything. Her face was growing paler. He was being cruel, he knew. Cruel to her, cruel to himself, but he couldn't help it. The anger he felt was crisp and real and at least kept the self-pity at bay. He drove in the left lane, fast as he could, headed down 280, over the rolling hills, back toward San Mateo. He felt like driving into a post.

"It's a money thing," he said. "It's easier for the police to call her death an accident. That way, they don't have to devote the personnel."

"Either way, we have to make arrangements," said Barbara. "We have to take care of our daughter. We can't just leave her at the morgue. Besides, you heard what the police said. It doesn't mean they have closed the investigation."

Nick had heard, of course. The whole goddamn story. They had done the forensics, they had done all the tests, and these tests were part of the permanent record in the event Angie's death was ruled a homicide and a suspect emerged. It was how things were done. There was no reason to keep the body in indefinite storage. The tests had been conducted, and the tests themselves served as the evidence, as the medical facts.

"But what if the defense comes in with some hotshot attorney and challenges the tests. We're supposed to rely on the SFPD? On their goddamn lab work and some scatterbrained cops?"

Nick had given the same argument down at the station, and the cop had sat there in silence, stoic as a rock. Barbara was quiet now, too, but she didn't have that kind of fortitude. He was wearing her down—refusing to let go—but once again he could not help himself. At the same time, though, he noticed the stubborn beauty in her face.

"I'm not putting Angie in the ground," he said. "Even if I have to pay the storage costs for thirty years, I'm not putting her in the ground."

He took the off-ramp too quickly, almost losing it. They descended onto Rancho Road, then wound around the hill back toward their house.

"I can't bear thinking of her in storage," said Barbara.

"The Italian oak."

"What?"

"Gucci's going to get the Principessa. From Italian oak."

"Yes." Her voice was resigned.

"I'm not burying her in some cheap fuck laminated box. Not my daughter. And she's not going in the ground until I know what the hell happened. She could have had this BMW if she wanted. Goddamn you."

"Yes. Goddamn me."

"I would have done anything for her."

His wife didn't respond. The line of her jaw had gone rigid. It was a hard look, one she did not show in public, cold and uncompromising. A look only a husband got to see.

"I would have done anything," he said again.

There was a plea in his voice, but it did not soften her, and it occurred to him that all these years, everyone else, himself included, had had it backward. She was the rock. He was the one being worn away.

Next to their house, on the other side of the oleanders, there was a fire road that went back into the open space—and as he swung the car around he happened to catch sight of a vehicle parked in there. A van, maybe. Teenagers, he thought. Teenagers parked behind the oleanders, making out, smoking dope, doing whatever teenagers did. Sometimes the kids wandered up into the hills, hooting and making noise all night, getting into mischief. Last time around he'd had to call the cops. Seeing the van now, for some reason, reminded him of the young woman with the clipboard, the solicitor whom he'd left standing at their door this afternoon. They didn't get many solicitors up in here, but either way she'd vanished by the time he'd returned.

Nick pulled into their drive and killed the engine. He and Barbara sat a moment in the darkness. The voices of the neighbors carried down from across the way, and closer by there was a skittering noise, a stirring in the gravel—but the hills were full of things, raccoons, burrowing creatures.

"Do you want me to come in?" he asked.

In a way, it was an odd question. He usually did pretty much as he pleased. If he was going to spend the night away, he did not ask her permission.

Barbara gave him a wry look, then climbed out of the car. It was not fair, that look: full of accusation, as if everything in the world were his fault. He felt the old desire to settle something with her—a desire best satisfied, he knew, by just driving off. She was at the doorstep now. He turned the ignition but in the glare of the headlights he noticed the gate to the backyard was wide open.

Teenagers.

He walked into the backyard, but everything was in order. Nothing had been disturbed. In fact, the yard had a serenity about it, here in the foothills, under the black sky, with the lanterns along the flagstones and the blue light emanating from the pool. The remote lighting was on inside the house, and he could see through the slider into the kitchen and the living room. It was like a picture in a magazine. Outside, there was no breeze. The red maple and the bamboo and the Mexican palm were perfect in the stillness. He remembered the excitement with which they had moved in, and those first warm days, his daughter and her friends lounging by the pool in their bikinis, with their long legs and their teenage beauty. Now Barbara was on the other side of bedroom slider, pulling shut the curtains. She saw him, he was all but certain, but didn't acknowledge his presence.

He took out his cell.

Anne Marie had left him a message earlier, about some final bit of paperwork from Prospero, regarding the Solano deal. He meant to call and tell her he was on his way, but he did not want to leave the backyard. It filled him with an emotion he could not describe. Sadness, yes, nostalgia, but something else—a sense of dread, maybe . . .

He noticed something then. The cat bowl his wife had placed on the diving board. It had been knocked over and the food was scattered. He had not noticed before, he guessed, on account of the pool lights and the angle of the board and the way shadows fell against the walk. He stepped toward the bowl. Shook his head. Then, all of a sudden, he sobbed. You close the biggest deal of your life, and your daughter turns up dead in the bay. He had bought the Waterhouse Building, put a second mortgage on everything he owned to get it. It should be a time for celebration, that clever bit of business. The deal had all hinged on Solano Enterprises. Solano's people had not put up any cash but agreed in advance to a ninety-nine-year lease that covered Nick's payments and left him free to develop the rest of the property. Office space was scarce, going up. There wasn't an extra inch in the city.

But now that deal was all signed, he'd begun to suspect it had been a mistake.

He bent over to pick up the cat dish and at the same time he glanced down into the blue water. What he saw then, lying in the pool, took a moment to register.

The cat.

Eccentric lay in the shallow end, not too far from the edge of the pool, in maybe a foot of water. The animal was white and ragged and looked like a stuffed toy someone had thrown into the pool.

His cell rang.

He was still new to the device and it rang four, maybe five times before he managed to answer. The difficulty heightened his panic, and the voice on other end, very cool, relaxed, heightened it yet more.

"Nick?" The voice was that of a young woman, speaking softly, and for an instant he thought it might be Angie. "Have you been out to the pool yet?"

"Who is this?"

Nick thought of the open gate again . . . the van around the side . . . the woman with the clipboard . . .

"Maybe it would be a good idea for you to call off your investigation. That's all I'm saying."

He heard a man's voice in the background, two men, maybe, laughing, stoned. The woman was not alone.

"Who—"

"And as for the cops, you know, how closely do you really want them to look? Just think about it, okay?"

The line went dead.

Whoever it was, they knew his cell number . . . They knew where he lived . . . They knew he was at home, they were watching the house . . . and just then Nick heard the van fire up, on the other side of the fence. He was tempted to chase it . . . tempted to call the cops . . . but something clicked inside him then. Since his daughter's disappearance, the dread had been growing, an idea beneath the surface . . . A couple of weeks back, he'd made a phone call on Smith's behalf . . . to La Rocca, goddamn La Rocca . . . And if he called the cops now . . . There was Barbara to worry about, there was Anne Marie. Soon he was on his hands and knees, peering over the edge of the pool. The water was shallow here, not even a foot deep. No, Barbara did not need to see this.

Nick rolled up his sleeves. He lay flat on his stomach and reached into the water. With one hand he took the scruff, and with the other he gripped the hind legs. The lifting was easy at first, but heavier once the animal broke the surface of the water. The cat had blood on his paws and shins. Its cheeks were abraded, too, and the upper torso. From trying to claw its way out, maybe, there at the lip of the pool. There was vomit on its ruff, and aspirated foam on its lips, and its teeth were peeled back and its eyes gone cloudy. Nick wrapped the cat in a piece of weed cloth and headed out the rear gate, down an easement behind the house. The path ran alongside a hill of high grass and oak shrub and anise weed. There was a ravine nearby, and on the other side of the ravine the hill sloped up to the freeway. In the daylight, the hillside had a gentle, rolling look, yellow ranch land overgrown with scrub oak and eucalyptus. Right now, though, the shape of the hill was unclear, and it was just a darkness looming over him.

Nick had at first intended to take the cat down to the ravine, but his shirt was soaked through, and suddenly he could not stand holding it close to him anymore. He waded into the grass and threw the animal in the high weeds behind an oak tree. Then he went back to the house and showered. It was a hard stream of water. He stayed under the spray until the water went cold and then he got out. His black polo was soiled, and so was the front of his pleated pants. He put the clothes in the hamper and stood naked, looking back through the mirror at his wife on the bed. Barbara was lying on top of the covers, still dressed, with a handkerchief over her eyes. He got some clothes. He put on a clean shirt and some pants and stood there looking at his wife. He still had not called Anne Marie. Perhaps he should not leave his wife alone.

"You blame me," she said. "But we both know the truth."

"Don't talk like that. This isn't anyone's fault."

She had not taken the handkerchief from her eyes, but when Nick took a step toward her, he saw her body stiffen, and in that stiffness was a lifetime of accusation.

"Go," she said.

Then Barbara stood up. She brushed past him on her way out of the room, but did not meet his eyes. Nick sat on the bed to lace his shoes. As he left, he could hear her in the backyard, calling the cat.

PART TWO

FOURTEEN

The light was too balmy, too beautiful. When the fog lifted, there was a hallucinatory light over the city. It built in intensity as the day went on. It was a lotus light, honey-colored, that at once filled you with desire and made the world seem an illusion—a balmy light full of suggestion. It was horrible, insufferable. It was gold light, a beautiful, divine light that made you feel as if you were standing in hell, looking though the window glass at a place you could never enter.

Dante crossed Stockton, into Chinatown.

The light was overhead here—playing off the balustrades, the faux pagodas, the ragged neon—but it did not reach to the streets, to the stooped women, all in gray, fussing over the vegetables, or to the old Chinese men with their berets and baggy slacks, their checked shirts and high-buttoned collars.

He headed across Market, to the Utah Hotel.

It was a long walk. Past the Third Street flophouses into the heart of SoMa—a warehouse district South of Market in the shadow of the Bay Bridge, where the old railroad lines gave out and there were still fragments of the turn-of-the-century neighborhood scattered among the concrete warehouses and glass storefronts and retro buildings converted to loft apartments.

Up Bryant, it was a wall of white noise.

The heart of the boom.

SoMa had been a residential enclave, grand houses on sloping hills. The neighborhood had drawn its wealth from the waterfront, but all those houses were gone. After the gold rush, the city engineers had plowed down the hills, laying it level, laying down a grid. A new neighborhood had been built on the grid, but most of that was gone, too.

The heart of the boom.

Giant pieces of white concrete, upturned rubble. Brick buildings torn in two by the crane.

The Utah stood up Bryant, in the shadow of the freeway—a surviving Victorian in gaudy Italianate. It did not appear quite real in the current light, but perhaps it never had. A small crowd mingled on the sidewalk—a hip crowd, paisley brights and slit skirts and heavy shoes with big soles. It looked like an art opening, but the murmur, if you listened, was of stocks, gainers and losers, of technology, of baud speed and platform and scalability. At the door, a young woman handed out the latest issue of *Wired*.

Everything has changed, the magazine proclaimed. The old rules don't apply.

Inside, the Wonder Lab from Menlo Park had a holographic display showing how computer gaming techniques would change the world. How it would soon be possible to conduct a war via remote control. How the terminally ill would store their brain waves on the Web and talk to their children from the grave.

If not true, it would be true soon.

Only the doubters would be left behind in this yellowing light.

Solano's group was on the second floor. There was a table at the front of the room and several dozen folding chairs, and behind the table a projection screen that was blank at the moment. After a while Solano came in, along with a handful of others. The audience craned about in their chairs. Bill Whitaker was on the program, but Dante did not know which of these people he might be.

Solano took the podium.

His manner was not so different from what Dante had observed earlier, self-assured, yes, but with a hesitancy underneath. His lips turned in that smile of his, a smile like cut glass, and his hair was mussed. Solano's eyes, though, had a certain fixity, and he possessed, in his gestures, the manner of someone who had penetrated an inner realm.

Solano's glance passed over Dante. If the man had seen him, Dante couldn't tell.

Solano began. His presentation was a recitation of names, spoken slowly, with an offhand charm. *Gutenberg.* He smiled to himself, as if he had a secret he could not reveal. *Whitman. Dinah Shore.* It was a ragged smile that suggested whatever you saw in front of you was only a part of what he possessed, that there were other things he was holding back. *Sigmund Freud.* That part of him mocked the very names—*Cleopatra, Che Guevara*—that he now mentioned, as well as the images on the screen behind him. *Fritz Lang.*

The juxtapositions were arbitrary. People of the sword, people of culture. *Mr. Ed.* Scientists with real-life entertainers and cartoons. *Katherine the Great.*

Meanwhile the screen filled with pictures, but the faces on the screen did not coincide with those of the people he named. *The Dalai Lama.* Rather they were faces of the anonymous. People at offices and schools. Workers on the job. They were not particularly stylish photos. They were instead somewhat mundane—*Bessie Smith*—the kind of photos that might be taken out of annual reports or school catalogues or brochures for the Water Department. Through it all was Solano's droll voice, somewhere between mockery and reverence.

Malcolm X.

On the screen the images no longer focused on individuals but groups, streets scenes, people in a crowd, the crowds growing larger, a sea of people—then zooming in—*Adam Smith*—tight focus, a solitary face that seemed neither man nor woman. Then a randomizer took over, taking the colors of that last, anonymous face, with no relation to the name he uttered, and scattering them over the screen.

"A lot of people," said Solano. "A lot us are working on a vision. One that breaks down the barriers between those who have access, between those who have the power of knowledge, and those who don't." The tone in his voice was ambiguous, so that you could not tell if he was making fun of those barriers, or those who wanted to knock them down. Then he was earnest. "This is not a vision I created. It's not a vision of one company, or one person. Our goal today is not to take credit but to let you know the contribution the people at our company are trying to make." He gave the crowd his smile again, and in that instant the fixity in his eyes gave way, revealing something beneath the surface almost, but not quite. Unhinge this world, Dante thought, and the man will fall apart. "Now," said Solano, "let me introduce you to our team."

Dante leaned forward then, looking to see which one was Bill Whitaker. But he was disappointed.

Whitaker was not here. Or if he was, he was not among the handful at the front of the room.

Solano fell quiet, and his underlings took over.

Solano Communications, they explained, was creating its own private communications network and the content to go with it. The goal: to deliver custom material to people in the workplace. Based on proprietary technology. Faster than the existing Internet. Drawing its material from archives that were growing exponentially.

An intuitive system . . . offering scalable solutions . . . interactive capabilities . . . operating on multiple platforms.

They went on, for Dante's money, a bit longer than he cared to listen. At the end, he knew little more about what Solano was doing, precisely, than when he had sat down.

Dante approached one of Solano's people: a young woman playing a role similar to the one Angie had played—a kind of press liaison who gave everything a down-to-earth spin.

"I was wondering if you could tell me how I might get in touch with Bill Whitaker."

"Bill couldn't be here," she said. "He's up against some pretty tight deadlines. But it if you could give me your name and number—"

"How about Jim Rose?"

"I don't know if we have anyone by the name."

"How long have you been working here?"

She looked at him blankly.

"Did you know Angie? Angela Antonelli?"

Solano appeared now and inserted himself between them. He had the faintest line of sweat over his upper lip, and his voice carried a chill.

"I don't know if this is the time," Solano said to him. "Or the place."

"I called your personnel office, looking for Rose. But I haven't had much luck."

Solano and the woman glanced at each other, and Dante saw something pass between them. He saw how this pretty young woman, with her red hair and her green eyes and her flame blue suit, was enamored of Solano—in maybe the same way Angie had been enamored—studying his face in a crowded room, looking forward to that moment later, away from here, when his guard fell and something was revealed, maybe, in the shallows of his eyes.

"How about Whitaker?" Dante asked. "When can I talk with him?"

Solano's presence had drawn a small crowd. Potential customers, perhaps. Investors. People looking for jobs.

"Yes," echoed one of them, "where is Whitaker? I was hoping to ask him a question or two."

"On deadline," said Solano.

The young woman leaned in to the group. "I'll have Bill get in touch with you," she said. Then she touched Dante. "And you, too. If you give me your card. I'll make sure he gives you a call."

She was lying. Whitaker was not going to give him a call. Meanwhile Solano had slipped away, separating himself from the crowd, and now he stood talking to a man across the room. The man was in plain clothes, but he was security, Dante guessed. Someone to keep troublemakers at bay.

Outside, the light was gone. The sky was black, and Dante headed through SoMa. There were some fashionable clubs South of Market, and some not so fashionable ones, too, but in between the blocks were long and the sidewalks empty. Dante knew this area from when he was a cop; out-of-towners would come to hit the clubs, then find themselves lost in the empty space. A couple of kids swaggered by as if it were 1980, done up in spiked hair and leather jackets, and some dykes hung out in front of a bar across the street. There were some hard cases sleeping in doorways, and ex-cons just off the bus from Quentin. Under the freeway, he spotted a deal going down and a gang of smokers hunkering in a circle. It wasn't grass they were smoking, and it wasn't crack, either. The ground was littered with foil.

He thought of what Barbara Antonelli had told him, about the mess on Angie's floor.

"Come on down here, old man. Come get some."

The man was a dealer. Dante could tell by the switchblade swagger, by the rotten teeth and the acne scars on his face. Dante felt the old ache inside himself. He felt the craving in his blood. He did not like to think much about the life he'd led those years he'd been away from The Beach, but the truth was he had not liked thinking about it even then, and he'd succumbed to certain temptations. He had taken comfort how he could. So there was a part of him now that wanted to slug the dealer in the face, but another part wanted what he had. Part of Dante wanted to be down on his knees with those Tenderloin junkies, those welfare moms, those runaways.

"What's the matter with you? You some kinda cop?"

"Yeah," Dante said. "I'm some kinda cop."

The dealer backed up. He laughed, ha-ha. Dante laughed, too. It took all his effort not to put his fist in the man's stomach, or bring an elbow around and knock out all his teeth.

He glanced at the foil.

He didn't want to think what he was thinking.

He headed toward The Beach.

FIFTEEN

Later that night, inside Angie's apartment, Dante once again went to the armoire and looked at her clothes. He thumbed through them as he had done before and found himself overwhelmed in much the same way. There was a certain perversity in it, he supposed, but it wasn't perversity alone that had brought him here. There were things that still rankled at him. The missing computer. The stained nightgown.

What had happened?

One explanation, he guessed, was that Angie had had the laptop with her that night she'd disappeared. Perhaps it had been on her arm, in its carrying case, and had fallen with her into the bay. He supposed that was possible. But there was something else that made him wonder otherwise. The way things were arranged haphazardly in the drawers. The dirty clothes on top of the clean. At first he'd thought it had been Barbara Antonelli, rearranging. But there was too much disorganization.

Someone had searched the place, maybe. Someone had torn it

up. But it hadn't been anyone professional, because they'd left too many traces.

The jism. The bottle of wine. The empty glasses.

He went to kitchen. Under the sink he found the wine bottle Barbara had mentioned. Now he took the rest of the trash can and dumped it out. Aluminum foil, burned at the edges. He unwrapped the foil and held it up to his nose. He recognized the smell. It was a smell he would have recognized even if he hadn't just been down there under the I-80 interchange.

And everything shuffled in his head.

Angie in another world. On her knees, like those people beneath the underpass. Angie bringing someone here to fuck. To get high.

Then stumbling into the water.

He went to the window and looked out at Mortuary Row. No, he thought, this didn't add up, either. Something else nagged at him, but he wasn't sure what, and then he saw someone lingering in the shadows across the way.

Whoever it was, they pulled away suddenly, and Dante bounded down the stairs. Moving too quickly, perhaps. Allowing himself to get carried away.

Jim Rose, he thought.

The alley was empty, but up Powell he spotted a figure receding, head down, a man the same size and build of whoever had been in the alley, maybe, he couldn't be sure, the same build as Rose, perhaps, but he didn't know that, either. He had only the one picture to go on, Rose leaning slope-shouldered against the boat railing Dante started after the figure, not running quite, but almost, closing the gap. Was it Rose? Yes! No! And when he was within hailing distance, he felt it a near certainty. A feeling based on instinct, on the swarming feeling in his gut. Then the man, hearing Dante's footsteps perhaps, glanced over his shoulder and started to run. Dante's certainty became absolute. He bore down. He grabbed the man by the collar and threw him against the brick. He was mistaken.

The man at his feet, lying on the sidewalk, was not the man in the picture. He was not Jim Rose.

The stranger rolled way from him then, yelling as he rolled, waving his arms and flailing in a manner so ridiculous, so ineffectual, that Dante wanted to kick him, to chase him down and stomp him until he was quiet. He'd felt the impulse before, back when he was a cop. He feinted now in the man's direction, but at the last minute held off. The stranger rolled to his feet and scampered down the hill.

Dante went the other way, up Powell. He needed to work the wildness out of himself, so he kept going, and pretty soon he was at the top, standing in front of the Stanford Hotel, the place where the cable cars crested before plummeting down again.

As he stood there, his cell rang.

It was Jake Cicero. Dante was glad to hear from him. There was something about his voice. The gruffness, the Old World fatalism.

"I got news for you," said Cicero.

"What kind of news?"

"You sound out of breath."

"I was just up at Angie's place."

"Find anything?"

"No."

"Then why are you breathing so hard."

"Ghosts," he said. "I was chasing a ghost."

Cicero laughed. Dante could hear the sound of smoke in his throat, like that of some aging nightclub performer. He could hear tinkling glasses and guessed that Cicero was in the bar by his house where he went sometimes when his wife wasn't around. Dante could hear the old juke in the background. Tony Bennett, he thought. Or maybe Dino and Frank, some kind of duet. The cell was fading in and out, picking up static, stray conversation, and it was hard to tell.

"How about Whitaker?" asked Cicero. "Did you talk to him?"

"No. He wasn't there."

"I thought he was one of the featured speakers."

"I thought so, too."

"Well, I don't know if it makes any difference now."

"Why not?"

"I just got a call from Antonelli."

"What's he doing, replacing us? We going too slow for him?"

Cicero laughed again.

"You got it half right, anyway. He's pulling us off the case."

"Did he give a reason?"

"He said it was too hard on his wife," said Cicero. "He said to let it drop. Let the cops handle it."

"I thought he hated the cops."

"Well, you know Antonelli, how he is, but I have to say . . ." Cicero's voice started to fade. The reception was breaking up. It skipped in and out, and by some anomaly the background noise was louder than Cicero's voice. Dante could hear Bennett on the jukebox now, singing the song everyone knew. The one about San Francisco and your heart breaking on the concrete. Cicero faded in.

"And it makes sense. Barbara and Nick want to bury their daughter. They want closure. They want to move on."

"Yeah," said Dante.

He was standing there on top of Nob Hill. It was the place in the city everybody talked about. The place where he'd kissed Angie once upon a time and other girls, too, whose names he could no longer remember. Meantime, Jake was still talking. Sounding a little drunk, saying this was how things went in this business. You followed a trail and then the client jerked the plug and you never knew. All this while the fog was coming in and Dante could see it rolling in over The Beach and up around the high tiers of the Bay Bridge. From this spot he could see down the hill into the gaudy nonsense of Chinatown, or the other way to Union Square, and at the same time taste the fog in his throat and feel the transport cable trembling in its groove under the street as the pulleys strained to bring the car up the hill. The phone was going in and out. He could hear the cable bells ringing and Bennett pouring it on. Then all of a sudden the static went away.

Dante dropped his voice. "I don't know if I can let this go that easy, Jake," he said. "I don't know." There was no response. "Jake," he said. And then he realized why the sound was so clear. The connection was broken. The line was dead. He stood there with the cell in his hand. The fog swirled low now, and a cable car lurched over the hill.

SIXTEEN

On a hillside, down the peninsula, a woman cried out, then cried out again. Perhaps her cries did not go unnoticed. It was dark, true, and there was no one on the street, and the neighborhood had, as always, the look of a place deserted. The neighborhood had this look despite the cars in the driveways and the lights in the windows. In the bushes, though, some small creature twittered at the sound of the woman's voice—a rodent, perhaps, a possum—and a shadow fell across a picture window. Up the road, a car rumbled into a cul-de-sac and disappeared.

It was a serene neighborhood, this hillside in San Mateo. The ranch houses were well tended. The birds-of-paradise were prim and upright. The televisions flickered. An orange dropped to the ground, thoughtless as a rock.

Meanwhile the woman called out.

"Oh, kitty," she called. "Kitty, kitty."

She went through a gate into an open area behind the house. She cupped her hand to her mouth and directed her voice up the hill, toward the junca and the oak. Then she went down the berm along the ravine, following a path behind the houses. She bent down. Calling into the gap under the redwood fences. Into the pink oleander. Into the poppies and scrub.

There was no response.

The woman was Barbara Antonelli, but she did not know how many of her neighbors recognized her voice, or even heard her at all. She had made a mistake, though, she was certain of that. The people inside the houses would tell you the same. You bring an animal to a new place, you keep it inside a few days. You let it out a little at a time, till it learns its way around. But she hadn't done that. She'd been foolish. So now the cat had scattered off somewhere, and she would never find it.

"Eccentric!"

Barbara stood at the top of the cul-de-sac. Her voice penetrated the stucco walls, she imagined. The neighbor could hear it in the garage across the way, his kid could hear it in the bedroom. His wife could hear it in the kitchen as she prepared dinner with the television on, the newscaster giving the local report, broadcasting the photos of the missing.

My voice is not just an echo on this empty street, lost in the wind and white noise from 280. Someone is listening, she told herself. *Someone hears. There are houses on this hillside. This is not just some canyon, filled with wind and rocks.*

Then she called out again.

"Kitty, kitty."

Barbara Antonelli shivered under the stars in her olive skirt and her sleeveless blouse. She went inside through the sliding door and lay on her bed. She was far above herself now, looking down. She knew how ruthless her husband could be, how self-absorbed. How foolish without thinking. But there was a moment you went back to, a million years ago, his body and yours, the smell of him as he put his arms around you, your skirt billowing, people looking as you strutted. There was the thrill you felt that first time you slid in the car beside him and the feeling you were safe, under wing, and pretty soon there were pictures in a drawer, furniture, and cloth and silverware, and your daughter racing down the hall "Daddy, Daddy," and the memory of his hip swaggering next to yours once upon a time, a dress you used to wear, a suit coat still in the closet, all those things that kept you in his bed, bound to him. Now something had happened, and she did not want to admit it, just like she had not admitted a lot of other things. But she knew. She lay in the bed in her olive dress. The pool was blue, and the only sound was that of a woman weeping. Faint at first, then louder. She rolled onto her side, but the wailing only got louder. There was no one listening, she knew that. There was nothing she could do to make it stop.

SEVENTEEN

The next day, Dante stopped into Prospero's Realty. He walked up the long stairs to the second-story office overlooking Stockton Avenue. At the top of the stairs, there was a dirty window that looked out into Chinatown—except it hadn't been Chinatown back then, when Prospero had thrown out his shingle.

Joe Prospero had founded the agency some forty-odd years ago, when the Italians had started leaving The Beach. It took up the whole floor now, and Joe had an office in the far back: behind the bullpen, behind the deal table and the water cooler—a traditional office with a glass wall and Venetian shades. A lot of the old-timers didn't much care for Prospero. They liked his handshake and his big smile well enough, but not how he ran his business. Or so they claimed. He hired Chinese agents. He had a branch agency called the Five Happiness that advertised North Beach properties abroad, to the Hong Kong market. He never let up with his leaflets and his smiles. No matter their complaints, Prospero was the one they came to when it was time to sell.

At the moment, though, Prospero was out. On the golf course, like he often was; and in his absence, his daughter Beatrice worked the desk. She was a blousy woman with a mole on her neck and hair the color of a pomegranate.

"Oh, if it isn't the Pelican," she said.

It was what the old ones called him, except Beatrice Prospero was not one of the old ones. She was no older than Dante, but she had adopted their manners. Beatrice resembled her father. In fact, she looked more like her father than her father looked like himself. She was thicker through the shoulders and had darker eyes. Her voice was different, though. Not high like his, but thick and throaty, sensual. She was almost attractive. Almost. And she had a way of looking at you, from the side, her eyes flitting from one end to the other like birds in a cage darting from one side to the next.

"I was looking for Marilyn," said Dante.

"Marilyn Visconti?"

"Sure."

"Oh, so the Pelican's looking for Marilyn Visconti? The man with the nose. The nose that knows. The nosey nose."

Beatrice said it with a wise guy glissando, like she knew everything that was up between him and Marilyn, all the secrets. Maybe she did, Dante thought. Maybe he should ask her and find out a thing or two.

"Yes," said Dante. "I am looking for Marilyn."

"You are interested in selling your father's place?"

"Not today."

"The market—it's so hot, the multiple listings burn my fingers." It was one of her father's lines, and she smiled when she said it. "These kind of opportunities don't come everyday."

"Where can I find Marilyn?"

"I'm an agent, too, you know." Beatrice eyed him provocatively, reared back her head. "Did you try her cell?"

"No," he lied. He had tried the number, but Marilyn wasn't answering. Screening him out. "This is something I want to talk to her about in person."

"Real estate's always personal. It's one of the most personal things I know."

"You're right," he said, and smiled despite himself. The Prosperos wore you down. "It's very personal."

"I mean—those people living in your house. Being a landlord. How long can that go on?"

"I don't know."

"I mean, is that you? A landlord? And that place you're living—with all that equity tied up in that house—does this make sense?"

"Probably not."

"Marilyn's a new agent. She's good, don't get me wrong—and of course, you two, well, you know each other. So there's a trust. But sometimes, with an agent, a little distance, it's a good thing. Better not to mix love and business."

"It's not the house. I'm not selling."

"Maybe not now." She shrugged. "But someday. How come you two don't get married?"

Her eyes were very bright now.

"That is a personal question."

"They're all personal sooner or later. But you know this, your line of work."

"Sure, I know."

"She's up at Marinetti's. There's a broker's open." She glanced at her watch. "Ends at three—but it's the first open. People linger."

"Thanks."

"You know where that is, Mr. Pelican?" Her voice was husky and sly. Beatrice Prospero looked at him directly then. She reminded him—with her floral blouse, her lipstick, her jewelry—of one of his cousins, big girls whom he used to fantasize about at night. She eyed him, reading his face. "Sometimes you move on. Sometimes, you just have to let go."

"Sure," said Dante. "I know."

"I don't think you do." Her eyes were very earnest. "Marilyn, maybe she knows—but I don't know about you."

Dante said nothing. Probably she was right.

"You want to sell that place," she said, and her smile was licentious, "you call me. I'll help you. I'll do everything I can."

She handed him the card then, though there was no reason. He had walked past Prospero's office most everyday of his life.

Marinetti's flat was on Weber Alley. In many ways, it was not the sharpest of locations. When Dante was growing up, these had been small flats for working-class families: plumbers, teachers, cops. Dante had been in them often enough. No views except the laundry lines across the airspace and a concrete patio three floors down, at the bottom of the fire well. There had always been plenty of noise, though: hollering kids and slamming pots and the guy across the way having some kind of tantrum against the wall. The narrow street was different now, at least on the face of it. The old lead-paint facades, gray and green and mustard brown, had been sandblasted and painted up in pastels. Also there was a phalanx of cars out in front of Marinetti's, double-parked. Mercedes and Jags and the big sports vehicles. The cars of Realtors all lined up, in the mute tones of silver and gold. An agent just now emerged from one such car, her heels clicking on the cobbled walk. She pulled on her skirt and gave Dante a small smile as she headed up.

The hours for the broker's open were all but over, but Dante could see people in the windows above. The door was open and at the top of the stairs he caught sight of Marilyn. Her dark hair was pulled back, and she was engaged in conversation with a man in a gray suit. The pair disappeared inside.

Dante had been up Marinetti's stairs before. He used to play here with Marinetti's twin boys. And he had climbed the stairs again, years later, when the daughter Gina Marinetti was married, and then again when the twins were killed in a car accident.

Upstairs there were maybe twenty, thirty agents, all lingering.

It was on account of the boom. Buyers outnumbered sellers. There was a shortage of inventory and plenty of money. On the fireplace, hundreds of Realtors had left their business cards.

Marilyn had dressed the place up, stripping out all of Marinetti's junk. The stacks of magazines were gone. So were the Italian knickknacks, the old photographs, the crucifix in the bedroom, the family heirlooms. The place had been made spare and relatively modern. There were flowers on the tables and a hundred colored pillows on the bed. It was hard to imagine Marinetti hanging around in here.

There were more agents in the kitchen, grazing at a courtesy table—laid out with food from Molinari's. This was where he found Marilyn, leaning against the refrigerator, talking to the man in the gray suit.

She met Dante's eyes this time, but did not hold the glance.

Dante remembered the kitchen. He remembered the twins elbowing one another—noodles up their nose, noodles in their hair—and he remembered Mrs. Marinetti in her red-stained apron.

Dante leaned beside Marilyn. The man in gray was talking about his client. "A software engineer." He dropped his voice. "Willing to match any offer." The man no doubt wanted the sale, but his voice was suggestive of other things as well.

At length, Marilyn turned to Dante.

"This is a surprise," she said.

"I just wanted to talk with you."

"You avoid me like the plague. Now you want to talk." She smiled when she said it, but Dante saw the flash in her eye.

"That's what happens you got a house for sale," said the man in gray. "People suddenly find you interesting."

"I'm not in real estate."

"That's what they all say." The man laughed, but Marilyn didn't. For this Dante was grateful.

Another agent approached. Dante remembered her from outside.

"Are you entertaining offers?"

"Not till Monday after next. We want to go through a couple of Sunday opens."

The woman did not look happy. She glanced around then, as if she knew better than to talk in front of the other agents but could not help herself. "My client wants to make a preemptive offer. He doesn't want to get into a bidding war."

"You can turn the offer in," Marilyn said. "But I can't guarantee."

"If I give it to you now, you'll just use it as a floor. You'll use it to bid the price."

"Would you do anything different?" said the man in gray. He touched Marilyn on the shoulder and let his hand linger. "Why don't we talk about it over dinner?"

"No," said Dante. "She's going out with me."

"I am?"

"Yes."

The woman agent did not know what to make of this conversation. She looked at Dante as if perhaps he were an agent as well. "All right," she said, "all right," but then her composure collapsed. "These bidding wars are obscene. It isn't right. Back in Spokane, I could buy an entire city block."

"You're not in Spokane," said the man in gray.

The woman stormed off, taking her offer with her. The man in the gray suit was amused.

"You'll be hearing from her. Don't worry about that."

"I'm not."

"And you'll be hearing from me, too. I'll give you a call," he said. He glanced Dante up and down, as if assaying the competition. Then he turned to Marilyn. "Wherever he takes you, I know someplace better."

So why have you sought me out," Marilyn asked.

"I wanted to see you."

"What for?"

"Old man Marinetti—it's going to be hard on him when he leaves that place."

"People like to say that," she said. "But a lot of times it's not so hard."

"I don't understand—if he's broke, why can't he just pull some equity out of the house?"

"It's not just the money."

"No?"

"He's morose. And sometimes—his wife, he sees her ghost, there in the apartment."

Dante had heard this before. Italian men and their ghosts. "He won't see her ghost at St. Vincent's?"

"Since when are you the defender of the aged?"

They were in one of the new restaurants, down off the square. It was a hot-ticket joint—one of those places Stella had complained about the other day down at Serafina's. The crowd was good—but not like it had been just a few weeks back, when the lines stretched into the street. Maybe Stella was right. These new people, they loved you for a little while, then they moved on.

But Marilyn liked it here, and the food was good. It had been a month, maybe longer, since she and Dante had been out together.

"You're right," he said now. "It's none of my business."

"Marinetti needs to live somewhere he can get assistance. He knows that . . . But you didn't ask me out to talk about George Marinetti. Did you?"

They'd known each other a while, Dante and Marilyn. Her family was from The Beach as well, and he'd known her almost as long as he'd known Angie. Angie had been the girl around the corner, with her lightness, her mercurial heart, and Marilyn was in some ways the opposite. More voluptuous by nature. More generous—and darker. She was seductive and unruly. Things between them had never been simple. And it had never been just the two of them, not for long. There had always been a third point on the triangle—a lover, an idea. As if they needed a centrifugal force to hold them in abeyance, neither too close together nor too far apart.

At the moment, it was the man in the gray suit, whoever he was. And if it wasn't him, it would be somebody else.

"You're investigating Angie's death?"

"Word travels fast."

"I guess it does."

"But it's not true. Not anymore."

"I don't follow."

"Antonelli pulled us off the case."

"Why?"

He explained it to her then, or some of it anyway. How Antonelli had hired Cicero Investigations to find his missing daughter. How for a while, after they identified the body, Antonelli had been convinced of foul play. He'd been pretty insistent. Now, suddenly, Antonelli had come around to the police view of things. Angie's death was an accident. She'd tumbled into the water and drowned.

"So what are you going to do?"

"Drop it," he said. "Leave it to the police."

"Can you do that?"

Dante lowered his eyes. She knew how he was. Marilyn had known him when he was with Homicide. He'd been unable to drop anything then, and there was no reason to think he was any different now. He did not let things go. He drummed his fingers, mumbling to himself, counting his digits, like they were beads on a rosary. When he was into a case—and he always was—he counted every crack in the sidewalk, every blade of grass. He dwelled in an obsessive netherland—contemplating witness memories, bloodstains, rumors. Always sorting, looking for the thread. Once he had thought—they both had thought—as soon as he solved this . . . as soon as the next case was done . . . But it didn't happen that way. There was always a loose end. An unexplained note. A scrap of cloth. A smear of blood that widened into a trail, and then vanished again, here in the neighborhood. But he couldn't let it go. In the end, he could not separate himself from what he was investigating. It had gotten him in trouble, this persistence.

"She was dating Solano, I hear."

"They had broken up."

"These things happen."

"I guess."

"It must be hard for the parents, though. I mean she gets drunk, she falls in the water."

"If that's what happened."

"You don't think so?"

"I don't know."

"If Nick Antonelli is willing to accept it, maybe you should, too."

Marilyn took a sip of her wine. She had never been one to be less than blunt, but he didn't mind that. She was a beautiful woman. She had untied her hair, and her skin had a flush, healthy look, here in the candlelight. Her hair had just started to gray, and you could see the white, the silver, mixed in with the auburn and black. The light pooled in her dark eyes, and he wanted to touch her face.

"I wanted to ask you something."

"Yes."

"Prospero Realty—they put together a deal for Antonelli recently?"

She nodded.

"Was it Beatrice?"

"No, no," she laughed. "This was old boy stuff. Antonelli worked with her father. He worked with Joe."

"I wondered if you know anything about that."

She gave him the look then. She pursed her lips and put her wine down. Those dark eyes of hers were even darker, and he wanted even more to reach across the table. To touch her. To not stop touching.

"So that's why you wanted to talk with me?"

"I don't understand," he said.

"It's just like you," she said.

"No, it wasn't that."

"I thought you were off the case. I thought you were done."

"Just table talk," he said. "Curiosity—it's only human."

"No," she said. "It's the dead. That's who you're interested in. That's all you've ever been interested in. Angela the beautiful. Angela the perfect." She snarled. "But let me tell you something. They're always perfect when they're dead."

She stopped then. He knew how Marilyn was. She let loose sometimes and you saw the heat in her, the quick flash. But sooner or later, she would come around. She wouldn't apologize, though. She never apologized.

They were quiet for a while. They drank their wine, they ate their food, and Dante could see the heat in her and feel the attraction between them. He had been with Angie when he was young, and that was one kind of thing, but Marilyn and Dante had gotten together when they were older, and that was something different. They were entwined in ways that were not so easy to unravel.

"Antonelli bought the old Waterhouse Building out in China Basin," Marilyn said at last. "The deal was just finalized."

Dante knew the complex. The place had been damaged back in the '89 quake—and had been sitting unoccupied for years. The site was unstable, and the building needed all kinds of environmental retrofit. It had changed hands a number of times in the last decade. The last owner had gotten part of the complex up to code, but had to bail out before finishing the job.

"What's he going to do with it? It's going to cost him a fortune to fix."

"There's such a shortage of office space—it's worth the investment now. Plus Antonelli's got some kind of deal with Solano Enterprises. They signed a long-term lease."

Dante remembered Barbara Antonelli had mentioned something along these lines, back when he first visited their house. Nick had looked uncomfortable and Solano, later, had skirted the subject altogether.

"My understanding, the computer business—the money's tightening up."

"It's just a blip."

"An arrow, straight up."

"Sure."

"Everybody gets rich."

"That's right. Be a cynic if you want."

Around them, voices were subdued. They were into prime time, but the crowd was slack. Not empty, but not what it had been these last months. The owner stood surveying the café, and though it had to be good in a way—a slow night now and then, a little time to rest, to work the back office—he looked disconsolate. Then the waiter came over to refill their wineglasses, and just for a minute, for no reason at all, Dante had a feeling like old times. Or what he imagined of old times. The world outside passing, all the moments slipping away, but here, now, at this table, this food in front of you, this drink, for a little while, you held the tide. That business outside didn't matter. Marilyn's face glowed in the candlelight, the passing shadows fell against the window, and for a minute, anyway, he was happy.

Afterward Dante walked Marilyn up the hill. The wind had picked up and Washington Square had gone cold. There was a smattering of transients on the grass, sleeping under cardboard, and a young Chinese couple making out on a bench. Across from Fior d'Italia, a street-corner preacher was warning about the end of time. How blood shall rain from the sky and the dead shall walk the earth.

"So," said Marilyn.

"Yes."

"What are you going to do?"

"I don't know."

"You don't have to walk me all the way," she said. "I can do it on my own."

Her eyes had an invitation in them, maybe, but there was also something else. A challenge. A demand. Before his father's funeral, he'd been gone a long time and things had gone cold between them. Then he'd returned, and he and Marilyn had gotten close again, and for a while they'd talked of selling the house on Fresno Street, maybe leaving The Beach, but in the end Dante couldn't do it, and he wasn't sure, really, that was what Marilyn wanted either. But there was still the question: What next?

He reached out and touched her face and wanted to walk with her on up the hill, but there was still the challenge in her eyes and also the feeling that never quite left him, that there was something just beyond the edge of his vision, something he could not quite see.

"I won't wait forever," she said.

"I know."

"The man in gray, the real estate agent?"

"What about him?

"He wants to fuck me."

Marilyn kept on up the hill. Dante watched her for a little while—how she diminished into the shadows—and he followed from a distance.

He stood outside her darkened apartment, looking up.

The light went on inside—and he saw her shadow cross the window and he felt some small comfort.

She was safe, anyway, he thought. He did not have to worry about her going for a walk along the pier.

On the way down the hill, Dante heard footsteps, but they turned away. Across the street from his apartment, two men loitered on the walk. Dante did the old tricks then, the ones he had learned during his time away from the city. He doubled back, then back again.

He walked slowly, he walked fast. He lingered by magazine racks and walked by Angie's apartment, and glanced down the alley where the night before he'd seen something move, and mistaken that movement for Jim Rose. There was no one down the alley now, and no one following him so far as he could tell. Still he could not shake the feeling, just as his mother had not been able to shake the necessity to climb the attic ladder. Down on Columbus, the two men were gone. Dante circled the block once more. He saw the blue van parked at the corner, but there was nothing remarkable about it. So he did not think anything of it, nor of the young woman in shorts and a peasant blouse, sauntering with her hands in her pockets, a cigarette hanging from her lips.

EIGHTEEN

Jake Cicero drove his Thunderbird through Cow Hollow. It was one of the new Thunderbirds, sloppy in the handling, floating over the street with a sense of indeterminate control. Up the big hills, then down—the vista wide in front of you just for a minute: the sailboats, the brown hills, the miles of stucco—and then down you went, wallowing into a dip. The car drove as if it were still 1977 and the streets were a million miles wide. It was a good ride. Cicero liked it. The T-bird was baby blue and it had a porthole in the hardtop.

His wife was on the cell.

"What are you doing?" she asked.

"Just a little bit of street work."

"I thought you weren't doing that kind of thing any more. Haven't you hired some other people to do that for you?"

"You know how it goes," he said.

Cicero considered explaining it to her. How Nick Antonelli had wanted him on the case so badly, then all the sudden changed his mind. But it wasn't just that. It was the fear he'd heard in Antonelli's voice—there underneath the belligerence. And now this man Whitaker, he was missing too. Cicero knew better, of course, than to let a case get under his skin, but there was still time on the retainer. In the end, he did not explain any of this to Louise. She did not care about the details. He had not married her for her interest in the details.

"I'll be home about ten."

"Did you look at the brochure?"

"Sure," he said. "I looked at the brochure."

He had, in fact, spent more time with the brochures then he cared to admit. The brochures, in some odd way, were what had inspired him to get out of the office and onto the street. Color pamphlets picturing couples at play. Young couples. Middle-aged couples. Men with just a spike of gray in their hair, women with their heads thrown back in a wild moment of laughter as they headed, arm in arm, down the gangplank toward the ports of call. Couples by the pool, water sky blue as could be. Pictures so crisp you could see the ice cubes in the glass and the erections under the men's swimsuits. Or lack thereof.

Better to be on the case.

"What do you think?"

"I think it looks swell," he said. "I can't wait." The truth was, no, he thought the trip looked like misery, and she could tell by the sound of his voice.

"Well, if you don't want to go . . ."

He hesitated. "Let's talk about it later."

"Okay—but I have to make some kind of decision. Life's not about chasing swine around the street," she said. "If I have to, I'll go alone."

"What do you mean by that?"

"Nothing. It's just I want to enjoy myself, that's all I'm saying. I think it's time. For both of us."

"I do, too, honey—I'm not saying . . . Honey . . ."

He was passing through the Presidio—six lanes of traffic merging in the inevitable swirl of fog on Doyle Drive, the on-ramp to the bridge; then the cell phone cut out, as it was prone to do down here.

"Oh, hell," he said, and tossed the phone into the empty bucket seat beside him. He knew Louise well enough to know that she wasn't going to call back. She was going to let him stew. And he felt the familiar, claustrophobic feeling he remembered from his other marriages—when you felt suddenly as if you were trapped inside a dark closet.

What was she up to? he wondered.

Cicero headed his T-Bird across the Golden Gate into Marin County. He had an address for Whitaker's ex-wife. The address was in Tiburon—and that usually meant certain things. The hills were covered with estate houses, and even the modest places, the little shoeboxes on concrete slabs, cost more than you wanted to talk about. Ann Whitaker didn't live in one of these, but she didn't live in a mansion either. She lived in a condo out at the point with a view over the water. It was a nice place, and she was a nice-looking woman, but in the end, it seemed, none of it had been nice enough. Whitaker had left her for a younger woman and a flat in the city.

"I don't know where he is."

"When was the last time you saw him?"

"He was here for the kids three weeks ago. Bill's supposed to take them every other week—but what else is new?"

The woman was a brunette in her early forties, thin and pretty except for her oversized jaw. Her clothes were expensive but on the matronly side, and her anger was apparent. Still, she had let Cicero in when he mentioned her ex-husband's name. Maybe because she was still attached to him in some way. Or maybe because any trouble of his was good news to her.

"He hasn't been at his job, did you know that?"

Her smile twisted. There was pleasure there, born of spite—but also worry. Mrs. Whitaker didn't look like she spent much time reading the employment classifieds, and no doubt the alimony was what kept her going.

"Who did you say you were working for?" Mrs. Whitaker asked.

Cicero explained. He was investigating the death of a young woman who had been involved with the president of her husband's company. Her ex-husband had worked closely with the dead woman. And now no one seemed to be able to find him either.

"Was he sleeping with her?" she asked.

"There's nothing to suggest it."

Mrs. Whitaker sat down. She put her hands in her skirt. Cicero noticed a small version of Mrs. Whitaker in the kitchen behind her—a young girl, maybe ten years old, with her mother's chin and the same puzzled, abandoned expression. Unlike her mom, though, the girl's hair was blond.

"He left two years ago—we had the biggest goddamn house on the hill—but he left, and now we're living here."

It wasn't exactly poverty, but he could see that she had taken a fall. Cicero started to feel bad, not so much for Mrs. Whitaker but for his own first wife, and his own kids. They didn't talk to him anymore. They thought he was the louse of the earth. Maybe he was.

"When was the last time you saw him?" he asked again. It was a habit you got into, repeating the question, because often enough the answer wasn't the same.

"Three weeks ago, like I said. Every other weekend, that's our deal. He was supposed to show up last weekend, to take the kids, but he didn't. Not a goddamn word."

"Did you call him?"

"Sure. I called his place in the city. And I called the cabin."

"The cabin?"

"Tahoe. It belongs to his family. The son of a bitch and his lawyers. I get the condo, the Mercedes. And he gets everything else."

"Nice car," he said.

"Yeah," she said. "It's great."

Her lips turned up and he realized he'd said the wrong thing, and he realized something else at the same time. Mrs. Whitaker—with her thin bones and her wide lips and her quick, distracted way of glancing about—had a resemblance to his first wife. His first wife had been born to wealth, or to the memory of it, and the two women had the same delicate arrogance.

"So he never called you?"

"Typical. He was working—caught up in one of his deadlines, I figured. That's the way it was with him. Devoted to his work. And whatever woman was worshipping him at the time."

The little girl, the blond miniature, stood behind her. She had a dour, somewhat confused expression, and despite her lace collar and her plaid skirt, she looked like she was ready to give something a swift kick. The couch. Her mother. Cicero himself. Meanwhile, from a nearby room, he heard the steady click of the computer mouse and a small voice yelping along with the animations.

"Go play with your brother," said Ann Whitaker.

The little girl went away, and it was just Cicero and Ann Whitaker. She wore her hair in a flip, a style that was both wholesome and out of date. Alone with her now, Cicero felt, suddenly, a hollowness in his chest.

"He always makes such a deal out of it when he comes by. Like he's the father of the century. But the truth of it, everything Bill does, it's all about him."

Cicero felt bad. He hadn't spoken to his own son in fifteen years.

"Well, at least . . ." Cicero said.

He fell silent, surprised at himself. He had been about to defend the man, maybe. Or to just tell her it wasn't so great from the other side either—but the woman glared at him, and Cicero knew she was right. You could come by every other night, drain your pockets, but it didn't matter. You had abdicated. Done it out of selfishness. For manly pleasure. For your dick. Or because you couldn't look at the lot of them without going out of your skull.

But it didn't matter the reason. You were the loser. You were the fuck.

"So you haven't heard from him?"

"Worse than that."

"Hmm."

"He hasn't sent the check."

"Which check?"

"Which check do you think?"

"Is that unusual, for him to miss a payment?"

"If the alimony's going to be late, he usually calls. He sweet-talks," she said. "I don't know why he joined that goddamn start-up. They don't pay him right; they defer payment with stock options. It was all about ego. About being the man."

She sat down and he saw it clearly. Married for fifteen years to this woman with the flip in her hair. To the pretty brunette who once upon a time had sighed when she touched him. Who had crow's-feet around her eyes and a bitter purse to her lips and two kids that left smudge marks on the walls. Sure, Whitaker had had his career and his family and his house on the hill, but the itch had got him. Young girlfriend and a job in the boom—why not take a chance and go for it? But the girl was gone, and the job hadn't panned out, and the family money had been divided. So now he had an ex-wife with a used Mercedes in a condo in Tiburon and two kids that would never really like him very much. And in that minute, for a reason he did not fully understand, Cicero felt a great attraction to Mrs. Whitaker.

"Where could he be?"

"Tahoe," she said. "It's his special place, like I said. He used to meet her up there on the weekends. Of course, it took me a while to figure it out. I thought he was working."

That's the way it happened, Cicero knew.

An earring under the bed. A negligee in the closet. A stain on the underwear. And then it all added up.

"He has a number up there?"

"The only way to get Bill is on his cell—and he screens those calls. Try him if you want; he's not responding to me."

She gave Cicero the number and he tried it right then. A recorded voice said the user had gone out of range.

"Who knows where the hell he is."

"You haven't called the police?"

"Why should I?"

"You might want to file a missing person report."

She blanched a little then. "As far as I am concerned, he's been missing a long time." She hesitated. "Maybe Jim would know."

"Jim?"

"Jim Rose. Young friend of his. Hotshot engineer from out east someplace. Bill lets him stay at his place in the city. You know he's a prince with total strangers—but his own family . . ."

"Jim Rose has been staying at your husband's flat?"

"Last I heard."

"I've been out there several times," he said. "There's been mail piling up."

"I think Jim's been working in the Valley," she said. "But he was there last night. And he called here, looking for my illustrious ex-husband."

Cicero fought back his excitement, tried not to let it show. He glanced at Ann Whitaker. She gave him her twisted smile, but she wasn't really looking at him. She didn't really see him. He saw the lost look in her eyes, something like grief, or sorrow. The little girl appeared in the hall, along with her brother. A feeling of great remorse came over Cicero. He smiled vaguely. Then he let himself out, leaving the woman alone in the condo with her two kids and the used Mercedes out front.

NINETEEN

The next morning, about ten o'clock, Jim Rose trundled down the apartment stairs, headed for coffee. Rose was unaware, of course, that Cicero and Dante were outside, watching the building. There was someone else watching, too, from the café across the street, but Rose was unaware of that person as well. Rose was thinking only of coffee. As he stepped outside, he caught in the entry the sharp smell of urine mixed with the morning air. There was a crack freak who stopped every night to piss in the security of the building's entry: long, luxurious pisses that in the freak's imagination vibrated with a sinister, yellow energy. Rose of course didn't know the addict's fantasies—only that the doorway smelled of piss, and that sometimes there was dark fecal matter as well, smeared over the aging marble entry.

Rose was growing a little weary of the city. Of its balmy light. Of its goofiness. Of its overpriced flats and the sense people had here that they were at the center of everything.

That San Francisco was the place. The only place. This was it.

Regardless, it was better than the South Bay. He had just spent the last week in Santa Clara on a high-paid consulting gig that had been supposed to last several months. They'd put him in a corporate suite down on the El Camino, expenses paid, then all of a sudden they'd gotten funny with him, like everybody was getting funny.

Money issues, they said. And they hadn't yet paid him the half of what they already owed.

So now he was back in the giddy city, unemployed.

Bad luck, he thought. Everybody else is rolling in venture cash, and I'm bouncing around. Going to miss the whole thing.

Rose had heard whispers. Things were shifting, the pendulum swinging. But there were always whispers. What troubled him more was the way no one returned his calls. Not even Bill Whitaker.

He wondered if maybe he'd been blackballed. If somehow Solano's people had spread rumors. Poisoned the well.

Such things happened, he knew, but he could not worry about it now. What he needed at the moment was coffee.

Coffee solved everything.

On the sidewalk in front of him were a half-dozen pigeons, scruffier and more stubborn than usual, refusing to scatter, absorbed as they were in a cinnamon roll someone had dropped on the pavement. As he pushed open the café door, Rose caught a glimpse of a man behind him. Where exactly he had come from, Rose wasn't sure, but he was at any rate an older man with a wild shock of white hair. He gave Rose a wan smile and didn't seem the slightest concerned with him. Another morning wanderer, after his caffeine.

Rose got his coffee and sat down with the paper. There was a story about a sudden slide in the market. There had been a similar slide about a month back, then a rebound—and now it was sliding again.

People were getting jumpy.

The place smelled of coffee, though, and that was good. Nonetheless, there was something off. Something had changed. Maybe it was his own perception. When he had come out from Cleveland, San Francisco had seemed wildly beautiful, flush with possibility, but now the bloom had faded. The young woman with the purple hair did not seem so much a hipster as she did a lonely kid, overweight. The man with the beret—openly gay, a queen who sometimes flirted with Rose, and just about anyone else who walked in—had developed lesions on his face. And the forty-year-old in the Buddha shirt pouring lattes behind the counter no longer seemed a free spirit, in search of transcendental karma, but a middle-aged loser, rooming in the Haight with kids young enough to be his children.

There were times, stupid as it seemed, when he felt himself longing for Cleveland.

Rose's eyes skittered over the other young men in the room, including the one with the beret, and he felt again the vague stir that had drawn him to the city to begin with. Though he hadn't known it then, or hadn't quite admitted it anyway. He sipped his coffee, and caught a customer across the room, playing eye tag, studying him in the window reflection—a little game Rose felt freer to play here in the city, though it still embarrassed him. Just as he was about to settle into it, the old man from the street slid in the seat across the table.

"Do you mind if I take this place?"

"No," said Rose, though in fact he did mind. There were other tables nearby the man could have joined. No empty tables, it was true, but why me? Rose wondered. What is it about my face that makes me look like somebody you can trust?

"My name is Jake Cicero," the old man said, and he slid a card across the table. Rose glanced at the card and saw the man claimed to be a private detective. "I wonder if you could answer a few questions."

"About what?"

He felt alarm, but also a surge of irritation. Another San Francisco crank, with an agenda, a game to play. Misfits masking as creatives. The city was full of them. Meanwhile, a woman seated at the front window glanced in their direction, looked away. She wore her hair in ringlets, and there was something familiar . . .

"This concerns a couple of friends of yours," said Cicero. "Angie Antonelli, and Bill Whitaker."

What came to Rose's mind then was Solano, and the mess there at the end when he'd left the company—and all the nondisclosure statements they'd made him sign. He'd heard stories about how companies pursued former engineers, harassing, intimidating.

"I don't know what you're up to," he said. "But I have no interest in talking to you."

Rose stood up. He didn't have to put up with this. He was angry at the notion people were snooping on him, and angrier yet when he reached the front door because he realized he'd left his coffee behind. Now he would have to go around the corner to another café to escape the old man, if indeed the son of a bitch didn't follow him.

I'll get an attorney, he told himself, *I'll* . . .

Outside, a stranger grabbed him by the arm. The stranger was not a big man, but he had an iron strength in his hands and pushed Rose hard into the doorwell adjacent the coffee shop. Then the old detective reappeared. They seemed to know each other, these two.

"We need to have a conversation," said the younger one.

Rose noticed the man's nose. He couldn't help but notice it. The man leaned fiercely into him, sticking his face into his own. The nose was jagged and sharp, and Rose feared for a moment he meant to jab it into his eye.

"Ease up," said the old man. "We don't need to do it this way."

The nose came closer. "That's right. It might be smarter to turn him over to the goddamn police."

"What are you talking about?" Rose asked.

"Angie Antonelli."

Rose didn't understand. The two men exchanged glances and there was a sudden shift. The old man intervened, put a hand on Rose's arm.

"You don't know?"

"He knows."

"Knows what?" asked Rose.

"Angie's dead," said the one with the nose. "Murdered."

Rose felt everything inside him go soft, but somehow he was still standing. Once again the old man intervened. "We don't have to do it this way," he said to his partner. "Young Mr. Rose here, he's upset. He was friends with Angie. He needs some time to take this in." Then he turned to Rose. "My partner, he knew Angie, too—and you gave him the wrong idea, how you ran off just now." The other man backed away and the old one, Cicero, started talking. He sensed the two men were working him, one against the other, but the old man's voice was soothing. "We can go down to my office. Not too far from here. Or we can go across the street to Whitaker's place—that's where you're staying, isn't it? Maybe you'd be more comfortable if we talked there."

Rose nodded. He wasn't sure why. Maybe because the old man had been nodding, and he'd imitated the action reflexively.

"I'd like my coffee."

"Sure, sure," said Cicero. "I'll go get it for you."

The other one stayed behind. There was something odd about him, something fierce. Rose was relieved when the old one came back, cup in hand, smiling. He put his hand on Rose's back and guided him across the street. In the window, the woman with the ringlets was watching. Rose was tempted to call out to her, to make some gesture, some sign. The idea of talking in Whitaker's, in familiar territory, off the street, had sounded good a moment ago. Now Rose had the urge to bolt, but he knew he wouldn't get far, not with the other one just behind, ready to pounce if he stepped out of line.

Rose took a last glance back. The woman in the window turned away, oblivious, but deliberately so, as if she were the one who did not want to be seen.

The three men were in Whitaker's apartment now, and Cicero stood in the bay window. There wasn't anything special about the view, or the apartment. It was the kind of bland, functional apartment that divorced men gravitated to, and there wasn't much to suggest that Whitaker had been living the swinging life after cutting the cord with Ann Whitaker.

Cicero drifted about the place. Meanwhile, he could hear Dante going after Rose, interrogating him at the table. Rose glanced in Cicero's direction, not wanting to be left alone, but Cicero ignored him. Cicero wanted to look the place over, and it made sense to let Dante talk to the man first, to do the softening.

Cicero took the bedrooms one at a time. It was easy to tell which was which. Rose's was the smaller of the two, and there was little in the room except for a futon and pile of programming books. Whitaker's room was a little more elaborate. He had a leather chair and an upscale wardrobe and a collection of jazz CDs.

From what he saw here, Ann Whitaker had gotten the better of the deal.

Cicero searched the bathroom then, opening the medicine cabinet. It was the grim bachelor stuff. He took a long piss in the toilet, then came out to join Dante and Jimmy Rose.

Rose looked glad to see him, but Cicero averted his eyes. He frowned and glanced at the floor. It was an act. He wanted to keep the man off balance. The truth was, he and Dante were walking a line here, playing it more like cops than PIs. Rose didn't have to talk to either of them, but he didn't seem to realize that. Or perhaps Rose was playing a game of his own.

"I need for you to go through this one more time," said Dante.

"I've already told you."

"I just need to hear it again."

Rose's coffee was gone now, and the young man drummed his fingers on the table. When they'd told him Angie was dead, his face had gone pale. Cicero's gut told him the surprise was genuine, but in matters of the gut, he knew, you sometimes went wrong.

"All right," said Rose, and he told his story again. The gist of it was pretty simple. There'd been a falling-out between the marketing department and technology, and Rose had lost his job.

"There was this moment, we were going through the specs, and I just had to say the truth: It can't be done. I don't think that in itself was any surprise. The surprise was that I would say it. I mean everyone knew. Meanwhile, the marketing people are going around, telling people we have these capabilities. But as soon as anybody asks for a demo—well, there is no demo. And there's only so far you can fake it. So, just as a matter of personal integrity, I had to say so."

"Who was in this meeting?"

"Oh, Solano, of course. Bill Whitaker. Angie. And some people from marketing. Sales types."

"What was their reaction?"

"Solano was cool about it. So the rest were cool about it. They nodded their heads. Then next day—Murphy in HR tells me to get the hell out. He comes to my office with a couple of security goons, and they have me sign about fifteen pieces of paper. I'm not supposed to reveal any technical secrets. But the joke of it is—there are no secrets.

"It occurs to me this is flat-out ridiculous. Because everybody in the company knows—because who the hell are they kidding. But they just wanted to keep the truth away from the venture people, just for a little while longer."

"Why?"

"As long as the venture people think you have something legitimate—and you can get the technical people to back you up—then they will continue to fund you. And there was another round of funding coming up. But from what I understand, all hell broke loose after I left that room. Because Whitaker—he wasn't going to play along either."

"Whitaker argued with Solano?"

"I mean, he knew better than anyone—and he was already looking for another job, like half the people in the company. And he didn't want to be lying about this, because he didn't want the stain. He has a reputation, you know. In the industry."

"So Whitaker balked, too?"

"Yeah, except that's a lot bigger deal than me balking. Because—you know—a lot of people look to him. We're at the beginning of a new era, you know."

"What era is that?" asked Cicero.

His voice was snide, but Jake couldn't help it. People had been talking about the new this, the new that, ever since he could remember, but as far as could tell, the operating principles were the same.

Put enough money in the air, enough fever . . .

"So where does Angie fit into all this?" Dante asked. "Was she fired, too?"

"No," said Rose. He hesitated now. "Her thing—with Solano, it was more personal."

"They were lovers. We know that," said Dante. "What was up between you two?"

"Me and Angie?

"What was up between the two of you?"

Rose shrugged. "We were friends, that's all. We talked. We confided."

Cicero cut in.

"Whose shaving gear is that in the bathroom?"

"Huh?"

"The Norelco. Also—the toothbrush. I noticed there was only one?"

"That's mine."

"So Whitaker—how long ago did he clear out?"

"I'm not sure. I've been working in the Valley, like I said. I just figured, you know, he went up to Tahoe. I called his wife a couple days back. Or his ex-wife, I mean. She had no idea where he was."

"Was there anything between Whitaker and Angie?"

Rose shook his head.

"You guys, that's all you think about. Who's fucking who?"

"Whom," said Cicero. "Who's fucking whom."

Cicero thought of Ann Whitaker and how cool she was, how diffident. The brunette had attracted Cicero, with her sharp features and her wide lips and her thin body, all bones and angles. Maybe it was her remoteness that drew him, or the vulnerability beneath the surface, but he now wondered what else she might be capable of. It could be he and Dante were chasing this whole thing in a wrong direction.

"The way I got the time line," said Dante, "you met with Angie the night before she died. You were one of the last people to see her alive."

"What are you talking about?"

"You called Angie's house Friday. You asked her to meet you. We've got records of this. We've got voice mail."

A shadow fell over Jim Rose's face. He was unshaven—an amber-headed guy with a Midwestern pompadour up front. He wore khakis and a pressed shirt and an alligator belt. He had a little bit of the hipster about him and a little bit of the hayseed—and a little bit of the guy with the slide rule. He wore black shoes and white socks, and though there was something unstudied about him you could see the intelligence there and the fact that he wasn't as frightened of them as he had been a little while before.

"Yes. I called her."

"Why?"

"We had planned to get together. I was just confirming. We did that sometimes. We got together for a drink. We talked."

"What kind of things did you talk about?"

"She was having trouble with Solano, you know. They'd had a relationship, and Angie had been pretty taken by him. Then the bloom came off—and, well, she saw him in a different light. The ethical stuff, trying to sell something that didn't exist . . ."

"So she broke it off with him?"

"I wouldn't put it that way. Solano broke off with Angie. He was the one . . . So I guess. I don't know. If the fact he was putting her out, if that was what made Angie see him differently. Or if, you know, it was the other way around."

"So that's what you did that evening? You talked about Solano?"

Rose shook his head. "No, we'd had that conversation a number of times. We were just getting together for drinks, down at Tosca's. As it happened, we didn't really talk much at all."

Rose went on to explain. He'd gotten there late and found Angie sitting at one of the tables with a couple of people in the business. Or Rose had assumed they were in the business: a rangy looking Englishman and a young woman with her hair in a fall. They weren't your typical types. At first he'd thought that Angie had known the pair already, but it turned it out they had struck up an acquaintance out of the blue. Max, the Englishman, seemed interested in Angie, and Angie was interested back. After a while, another man had joined the party, an older fellow, and Rose had used the opportunity to slip out.

"These three people, what did they look like?"

Rose described them the best he could. The woman with the fall was wearing pretty expensive clothes, hip, sort of, but with a corporate edge, like she'd just gotten off work. He couldn't remember her name. Lydia maybe. The Englishman was a thick-shouldered guy, with his hair buzzed short. The third man was thinner, older. Emaciated and sleepy-eyed.

"After he joined the table, I slipped away. I whispered good-bye to Angie, and I left. Angie was having fun. The group, it was a little rough around the edges, but you know . . . Angie has that about her. I mean— She was attracted to that kind of thing."

"Why did you leave?"

"Like I said, they were a little rough around the edges. And I had someplace I wanted to be."

"Where was that?"

He hesitated. "Tommy's place. Down in the Castro."

"You and Angie, you were friends? You confided in one another?"

"Sometimes."

"What kind of things did you tell her?"

"I'd rather not talk about that."

"Were you in love with her?"

"No." He laughed. "I already told you that."

"What did you talk to her about then?"

He hesitated, then let out a sigh, a shake of the head. "It may seem quaint in this town. But I haven't decided yet if I am out of the closet. Angie, she was somebody I could talk to that about." Rose smiled. It was self-conscious smile, a bit uncertain though not without irony. "Except now, I guess, I'm coming out to you."

"I guess you are," Cicero said.

"How about Whitaker?" asked Dante.

"What about Whitaker?"

"Is he gay, too?"

Rose smiled again. "Not that I know of."

The questioning died there. Cicero looked at Dante. He wasn't satisfied, and neither was Cicero, and he began to suspect maybe Rose was holding back on them, there was something he wasn't telling.

"Did Angie have her computer with her?" asked Dante. "Her laptop. Was she carrying some kind of case?"

Rose shook his head.

"No," he said. "Not that I remember."

After they were done with Rose, Cicero and Dante went down to the bocce courts on Columbus, behind the North Beach Library. There were other, better courts out in the Marina, but Cicero liked the one in the old neighborhood, secluded behind the chain-link fence and the ivy. The court was in poor repair, sure, but it felt more like the old world, like you were playing in the dust and the sand of some backwater village. Every once in a while, one of the old players still showed up, but not so often anymore.

Dante had been joining him recently.

He wasn't much of a player, but it didn't matter. Cicero enjoyed beating him. Today, though, Cicero was off his game. He had his practice set with him, the metallic balls and the retrieval chain. He had gotten the chain on account of his back, so he wouldn't have to stoop to pick up the balls, and he had become pretty adept with it lately, walking past the ball and dropping the magnet between his fingers, snapping the bocce back like a yo-yo on a string. They took turns for a while, warming up, then Dante put the jack ball into play, the pallino, and Cicero followed with an off-line roll. It was not so bad, not so good. Cicero lit a cigar. Sometimes he played better with a stogie in his mouth.

"My wife wants me to retire."

"Can you afford it?"

"She *thinks* I can," he said and laughed.

If she had any misconceptions, though, they were his fault. On account of things Cicero himself had told her, back when they were courting. Exaggerations about his net worth. "She wants me to fold it up and go on a cruise."

"That might be the thing to do."

"What makes you say that?"

"A man your age," said Dante. "I could see it."

"You're a jackass."

Dante took his turn. It was a two-step toss, not exactly pretty, a hard throw designed to knock Cicero's lead ball out of position, but Dante's foot slid past the foul line. The shot was lost.

"Did you think Rose was telling the truth?"

"Mostly," Cicero said. "But I've been fooled before."

"The thing that puzzles me is the computer. If Angie didn't have it with her, then where is it?"

Dante told Cicero about the mess in Angie's apartment—and the foil with its chemical stink. Heroin, he was sure. It was possible, he supposed, that Angie had brought the three strangers back with her from Tosca's. It was possible they'd gotten doped up together and gone out again later.

"The toxology report, though, it came up blank."

"Those reports aren't always correct."

Cicero went into a deep crouch, deep enough so that it hurt his knees, and he pushed a slow roller through the middle of the pit, toward the jack ball. It was good enough, but no beauty. He took the cigar out of his mouth, then went over and sat next to Dante on the bench. Cicero reached into his shirt pocket. He handed Dante a photo of Whitaker he'd pulled off the Internet.

"Ordinary-looking guy."

"We're all ordinary looking," said Cicero. "I've got the address of his cabin in Tahoe. His wife gave me his cell. But he's not answering."

"So what are you saying?"

"The wife, she filed a missing person report this morning. I am going after his credit card records. See if we can find out where he's been."

"Is she willing to pay us?"

Cicero shrugged.

"I thought you said Antonelli was finished with us. I thought he was pulling the plug."

"I still have his retainer," said Cicero. "He signed a contract. We have an obligation to give him his money's worth, whether he wants it or not."

"Something's in your craw."

"I guess so."

"What is it?"

Cicero hesitated. He didn't know how to answer that himself. He thought of Ann Whitaker again, of her two little kids. He thought of his wife, Louise, with her spinning classes and her trainer and her walking tours around the city and her sailing classes and her obsession with this cruise. It had always been this way. You had one life, but there was always another that beckoned. Another life beneath the surface of the one you lived, and people like him, fool that he was, he couldn't help but pursue. You would think he would know better by now.

"Why don't you hook up with Visconti? She's a good-looking woman."

"Changing the subject, aren't we?"

"Possibly, but I'm the boss. What's up between you?"

"Everybody's been asking me that lately."

"What's the answer?"

Dante sat with his fingers laced together and his long nose pointed at the ground. Cicero followed the slope of the man's nose down to its bulbous tip and it seemed to be pointing to the jack ball out there in the dirt. After a while, it became plain he wasn't going to answer.

"Maybe you should have a life for yourself," Cicero went on. "Maybe it would be good for you."

"Maybe you should go on that cruise."

Dante got up and tried another throw. It was a clumsy throw, a jackass throw, really, graceless as hell, but the ball rolled up close, and took the lead position. It doesn't matter, thought Cicero, I can do better. I'll knock it away. "Antonelli was tied to Solano's business some way," said Dante. "Maybe there's a connection there."

"To Angie's death?"

"To something. I don't know."

"Maybe someone scared Antonelli off. Maybe someone didn't want him to investigate anymore."

"Could be," Cicero said. "Could be the guy just wants to bury his daughter."

Cicero tried to imagine himself there on that boat. In that deck chair, feet up. Dozing off. All around the sound of the gulls and the blue water and some little island off there in the distance. The sun shining down, warming his face. When you got to port, there were charters. Smaller boats that took you into the reefs, where you could drop a line and pull up anything you wanted. Except what came up, in his imagination, was not some goddamn trophy fish.

"I want you to go up to Tahoe," said Cicero. "I want you to go up to Bill Whitaker's cabin and see if you can find him."

"Are you sure?"

Cicero nodded. Dante sat down once more on the bench, silent now. Thinking about that stinking foil, Cicero guessed, trying to imagine those people in Angie's apartment, wondering about her computer. Obsessive son of a bitch. Meanwhile, on the other side of the fence, Cicero could hear some Chinese kids playing and a mother scolding them. You could sit here for a long time before someone comes through that gate to play bocce, he thought. No one played this court anymore.

Maybe I'm done with Louise, he thought. Maybe that's what's in my craw. Maybe it's the Whitaker woman.

Maybe it's the dead girl they pulled from the bay.

He dangled the drop chain between his fingers. Maybe I'm just afraid to die. Maybe that's why I can't let it go. He let the magnet hang. Then he snapped up the steel ball and contemplated his roll.

TWENTY

Dante took the trip up to Tahoe. It was some five hours from the city—a drive across the Central Valley that took him through tule land and cottonwoods, past the buff-colored houses and the Sacramento subdivisions that sat now on the old arroyos. When he was a kid they would take Highway 99 through Concord and Marysville, past the prison in Vacaville, then to Walnut Creek, until the groves gave way to tomatoes and grasshoppers and it was nothing but heat pouring through the open windows all the way to Sacramento. It was a quicker drive now, and more comfortable—in his air-conditioned Honda—but it was also uglier.

More than once along the way he stopped, ostensibly to get gas, to take a leak, to smoke a cigarette in the dust by the side of the road. In truth, it was his old habits getting the best of him. Looking back to see if he was being followed.

As far as he could tell, he was not. There was no one.

He got back into the Honda. He climbed for a while. Into the Auburn Hills. Then into the Sierra.

Then down again, following the Truckee River into the Tahoe Basin.

Dante arrived at Whitaker's place in midafternoon. It was a little cabin in Tahoe City about fifty yards off the water. It was an A-frame, nothing fancy. The deck and the stairway were covered with pine needles and there was mail in the box. There was no car in the driveway, and it didn't look as if anybody had been around for a while. He considered taking a closer look, but there was a yard-man across the way who didn't seem to have anything to do but look in his direction. So Dante walked up the road a little ways and took a path down to the lake.

The lake was quiet, except for the sound of a speedboat across the water, on the Nevada side. The sound was muffled and remote. The lake spread out over the basin, and reflected the mountains in the gray water. The forests were redwood and pine and they obscured the buildings along the shore, all but the casino, which was somehow both tall and squat and rose well above the tree line. The opposite shore was farther away than it looked. Tahoe was the largest freshwater lake in the west, or so they said, and the vast, colorless plane of water played tricks with the eyes, deceiving you as to distance and size, in much the same way the desert might deceive you, or a great expanse of snow.

Out on the lake, a speedboat moved slowly toward the casino. The sound of the motor was distant, like that of a gnat drowning in the water.

Dante went down the path, back the way he had come. On the way past Whitaker's place he noticed one of the window screens was torn and the window itself sat crooked in its track. The yard-man across the street was still at his job. Dante gave the guy a nod and drove away.

Before he'd left San Francisco, Dante had gotten some information on Whitaker's expenditures these last weeks. The former VP and head engineer's last withdrawal had been for six hundred bucks from a cash machine in the casino about twelve days back, not long before Angie disappeared. Whitaker had used his credit card once at the casino as well, at the Lookout Grill—and another time at a bar in Tahoe City. Then he'd used it again later that day at the rental dock. After that both accounts went dark.

Dante drove around the lake to the casino. He'd gotten the location number of the ATM and it turned out to be in the card room, not far from the blackjack table. That made sense to Dante. Whitaker knew numbers, and blackjack was the kind of game you could get a system and do pretty well, if you knew how to hop tables and avoid moving your lips while you were counting.

Dante showed Whitaker's picture to casino security. Ordinarily security had no tolerance for private dicks, but Cicero knew the head guy, and the man let Dante talk to the table dealers. A couple of the dealers recognized Whitaker's picture. He'd been playing the tables for years. Had a cabin down the road. Played in spurts, usually alone, a win-some, lose-some kind of player. The last time anybody had seen him was a few weeks back, playing with some young woman. Dante showed a few more pictures, one of Angie, the other of Whitaker's ex-girlfriend that Cicero had lifted from Whitaker's apartment when they'd been grilling Rose.

The dealers couldn't place either woman and sent Dante over to talk to a bartender named Leroy Pink. Pink worked the Lookout Grill, which was not a grill so much as a counter overlooking the casino floor, and he knew most of the regulars.

"Oh, Bill Whitaker—yes," said Pink. He was a man in his early sixties whose nose was of such a color that Dante wondered if this was where he'd gotten his surname.

"Did he have anyone with him?"

"Bill Whitaker always had someone with him. He'd drink, he'd hang out."

The story didn't exactly match what the dealers had said. Dante showed Pink the pictures of Angie and Whitaker's girl, same as he'd shown the others.

"Neither of them," he said. "Those two are blondes. And the woman he was with, she was no blonde."

Angie wasn't a blonde, either, but Dante didn't argue.

"What color was her hair?"

"Brunette," he said.

"What did she look like?"

"Nice-looking. So what is this, you working for the wife?"

Dante didn't say anything. He just shrugged, as if maybe it were true—and let the guy think what he wanted.

"I thought Bill Whitaker was already divorced."

"He is."

"Then?"

"He's missing. People are worried."

Pink pushed out his lip. "What day did you say this was?"

Dante gave him the date and time. On account of the credit card, Pink was able to get pretty specific, down to the drinks they had ordered. A mai tai and a bourbon.

"So, what do you remember of this girl Whitaker had with him? What did she look like?"

"The blonde?"

"I thought you said she was a brunette."

"She had a nice ass. I remember that."

"Nothing else?"

"If she was with Bill, she had a nice ass." Pink rested his hands on the bar. "You get to a certain age, a certain station in life, you don't pay much attention to anything else."

Dante got back in his Honda. It was an unobtrusive car, not too clean, not too dirty, a straight-up Accord, a few years old, with nothing about it worth remembering. He appreciated the anonymity of the car and kept the radio off as he drove, his eyes on the highway, on the pullouts and the dirt roads, and on the cars behind him. It took Dante about forty-five minutes to get around to the other end of the lake, back to the California side, and locate a lounge where Whitaker had spent about fifteen dollars, according to the credit card company.

Enough for two drinks, Dante figured.

A mai tai and bourbon, as it turned out. He showed the pictures again but got nothing for his trouble. Then he walked over to the rental dock. It was across the highway, down in the cove.

The owner was working the dock and he found the invoice pretty easily. Dante showed him the picture of Bill Whitaker.

"Do you remember him?"

"No, I remember the boat." The owner shook his head. He looked at the receipt. The way the man looked, he could have been Leroy Pink all over again, except his nose had a few less veins. "It was two weeks ago, we had to retrieve the boat. Son of a bitch left it out in Rich's Cove."

"What happened?"

"The kind of thing that happens every once in a while. Somebody rents out a boat. They get shit-faced, or lost out on the lake, and they just leave it on the shore. Usually, they come back, they tell us. But sometimes they don't bother."

This didn't sound like Whitaker, at least not from what Dante had heard. Whitaker was a Tahoe hand, knew the lake. Unless, like the owner said, he was shit-faced. Or distracted by the girl.

"So what do you do, a case like that?"

"We charge the credit card."

"You don't call the police?"

"If every rental outfit called the cops every time someone ditched their rental material— I mean, that's what the deposits are for."

"Do you know who he was with? Does it say on the invoice?"

"No."

"Was he with a woman?"

"You'll have to ask Sal, the boat boy. He's the one who helped them. But he's not going to remember much. Unless the girl's sixteen years old, he don't pay attention."

"Where is Sal?"

"Day off. He'll be by tomorrow."

Dante stopped at a station and got directions to Rich's Cove, just so he could get a look at where Whitaker had abandoned the boat. By the time Dante got there, the sun was going down. The lake was darkening and quiet, and just looking at the water, it didn't tell him much. He thought of going back out to Whitaker's place. It would be easy enough to break in, but it was night, and he figured he would raise less suspicion in broad daylight. He would be better off parking the car out front in the middle of the day, rather than fiddling around in the dark. By tomorrow, too, the yardman would likely have cleared out. So Dante drove back to the Nevada side and checked into a hotel. It was a midrange place, relatively subdued: a card room and some slots and a roulette wheel drawing modest action. His room was up top, and the neon sign crackled outside his window. He pulled the blinds and slept. Sometime after midnight he heard a ruckus out in the parking lot. The happy shrieks of some drunken winner, or maybe some loser, it was hard to tell. Either way the noise did not last long, and Dante fall asleep to the sound of the neon crackling in its glass.

Dante headed back the next day to Whitaker's place. The location had seemed remote yesterday, but today it seemed more ordinary. Whitaker's cabin was in a cluster of similar cabins down a private drive, most of them built as second homes in the seventies, small places on odd-shaped lots that shared a rock beach with a view of the water. Dante parked out front. The yardman was gone and the street was empty.

Dante rang the bell, not expecting anyone to answer, and no one did. He tried the front door, just in case, then walked around to the torn window screen. Someone had been here before him, maybe just Whitaker, of course—having locked himself out, then forced his way back in—but either way the damage was relatively recent. The window screen was torn, yes, but there was no sign of rust, and the slider was still bent in its frame. It was a simple matter to wiggle the latch and climb through.

Whitaker kept a neat house, but it was a bachelor's kind of neatness, with a veneer of dust. There was a book by the bed, and a pair of slacks folded over a chair in the bedroom, and some other items here and there—like maybe he'd gone off unexpectedly. Otherwise the place was pretty much in order, and no doubt there were a hundred other cabins just like this around the lake, part-time residences with field mice in the walls and milk going bad in the refrigerator. Dante stepped outside onto the deck and looked across the water at the casino, same as he had the day before. It was the same scenery, just a different time of day.

Then he heard a car pull up out front. It was a patrol car, and the cop nuzzled its bumper close up behind Dante's Honda under the redwood tree.

The cop spotted him.

"Is this 419 Lakefront?"

Dante nodded his head.

The cop seemed at odds at what question to ask next.

"Is this your house?" he said at last.

"No," said Dante. "I'm a private investigator."

Dante handed him his card.

"What were you doing inside?"

"Looking for a man named Bill Whitaker." That part of it was true enough, but the next part, he stretched. "Alimony case. I'm working for the wife and she asked me to come up to the cabin here. Apparently he thinks it belongs to him."

"Well, I don't think she's going to be getting any alimony real soon."

"No?"

The cop hesitated. Pursed his lips.

"A couple of hours ago. We pulled him out of the lake."

It took a while for Dante to disentangle himself. From what he could tell, the cops were pretty much of the opinion that the death was just one of those things, guy gets drunk, slips off the boat.

Whitaker had been in the water almost two weeks, apparently; but they'd identified him easily enough, from a license in an inside pocket. The cops hadn't figured out yet that the boat had been a rental, or that there had been a woman with Whitaker on the boat. There was a chance, of course, they might not figure these things out at all. Even so, Dante beat it around to the other end of the lake to talk to Sal, the dock boy, to see if he could get a description before the police came knocking.

Sal was a dopey kid, like the owner had said, but Sal remembered the missing boat and the couple that had rented it. Or so it seemed.

"She was pretty old," the kid said. "Not so old as the guy, but you know."

"How old?"

The kid hesitated. "About thirty."

Dante thought to give the kid a lecture on the nature of age, but why would anyone want to listen to that?

"What color was her hair?"

"Brown." Sal spoke more firmly now. Then he touched the bill of his cap and peered out across the immensity of the lake. He toed at the ground. "Or maybe red. I don't know. She had it all tied up in a scarf."

TWENTY-ONE

Earlier that morning, a young woman by the name of Sylvia had spent several hours sitting in the café across from Bill Whitaker's place, on the lookout for Jim Rose. Sylvia had met Rose once before but, today, like yesterday, she wore her hair in ringlets and did not much resemble the woman he had seen maybe ten days ago for fifteen minutes in Tosca's. Anyway, Sylvia did not plan to talk to Rose. She was only watching at this point, trying to get a hold on his habits.

People were like clocks, Sylvia had learned. They went around in circles. Study them for a little while, and it wasn't hard to figure out where they'd be next.

Sylvia had learned this bit of wisdom from Arturo, her mentor. Arturo knew all the tricks, and he had taught them to her like you would teach a daughter, but he'd been slipping, she knew that. And now he was late. He and Max. The two men were supposed to have been here an hour ago, with a little something to tide Sylvia over—something to kill the dull hours—but they were not here and her body was beginning to ache.

Still, Arturo was a pro. He'd taken her off the street, taught her everything. Before Sylvia had met him, Arturo had worked with his wife. The pair of them, husband and wife, had never been caught, and they'd never made a mistake. And they never carried guns. Drowning accidents, that was their specialty. In the swimming pool. The bathtub. The Jacuzzi. But when Arturo's wife died from ovarian cancer, he'd needed someone to take her place. Someone to play the seductress. To befriend a lonely woman. To drop the GHB in a glass. It was a subtle thing, different every time, an interplay between two people, a dance with Arturo in the wings, watching, waiting.

Sylvia was grateful to Arturo. She enjoyed it, playing the part. Dressing up. Getting herself teed off in advance, finding the right buzz. Then after the gig she could just disappear. Hotel suite at the top of the Mark. All the high she wanted. Everything delivered. She and Arturo naked on the silk sheets, watching television. Maybe he put his hand on her breast once in a while, but it wasn't the way it seemed. It was more a father-daughter thing.

But now, there was Max.

A new element. Wild, fucking Max. You have to keep fresh, Arturo had said, and Max adds a new dimension. The truth was Max had been foisted on them. Because Arturo was lost in the fog. Because his wife was dead and he wasn't able to hold the balance anymore. Because he was using the needle, and "the Agent," as Arturo called him, the man in charge, the one with the clients, was worried about the future.

As for this job . . .

The business at the lake had gone smoothly enough. The guy Whitaker had all but rolled himself off the boat. But here in San Francisco, things had gotten sloppy.

Max's fault.

Or maybe her fault. Because she had started fucking Max back in Tahoe. Because she laughed when Arturo got all drifty and sentimental, talking about his years as a kid here in the city. Going on, tears in his eyes, about a little dog that used to follow him on the streets of North Beach.

She felt torn.

Then two things happened at once, more or less at the same moment.

Max and Arturo came around the corner in the blue van. And Jim Rose emerged from the apartment building across the way.

Jim Rose had decided he wasn't going to stay at Whitaker's anymore. He had his backpack with him and was headed over to the Mission. He had some friends over there, sharing a house, and he thought maybe he could stay with them. Rose was afraid the detectives who had cornered him yesterday were not done with him, and he did not really want to talk with those two again. He half-feared they might be tailing him. As he left the apartment, he noticed a woman emerge from the café. The woman in ringlets, he thought. When Rose turned again, though, she was gone. On the bus, no one seemed interested in him in the least.

He got off on Mission, out on Twenty-fourth, and headed into the Latin Quarter. The streets here made him uneasy. A lot of young hipsters were moving down here supposedly, buying places and fixing them up, but you couldn't tell at first glance. The streets were colorful, sure: murals and decaying Victorians painted up like it was fiesta time, Latino music blaring from the little shops and *tiendas*, but himself, he did not feel easy. A group of teenagers were hanging on the corner ahead, posing and leaning against a grocery wall. Maybe they were gangbangers, maybe they were just kids. Either way, he crossed the street to avoid them.

Rose turned the corner opposite the Aztec Grocery and looked for the address. He cursed the detectives for driving him out of Whitaker's apartment, and cursed his friends because their place was so goddamn hard to find. Meanwhile a blue van appeared on the street.

He found his friends' place. Or what he thought was their place. There was no number on the door, but the house was the right color, in the middle of the block, like they had said, with the scallops over the porch.

There was no answer.

The detective, the one with the nose, had described Angie's corpse for him. Told him how the cops had pulled her out of the water and laid her on a morgue slab with her designer skirt hiked up around her legs.

Rose left the porch now and went around to the back of the house. He tried the back door, but there was no answer.

He wondered who the two detectives were really working for. Maybe he was being paranoid, but there was a lot at stake these days. Part of him couldn't help but think this somehow went back to Solano. Companies could be funny about proprietary information, especially in this kind of environment, when the tiniest little thing could give a competitor an edge, and there was so much venture money at stake. Carried away in the moment, he had talked too much to the detectives, maybe, but he hadn't told them everything.

He had not mentioned Angie's journal.

According to what Angie herself had told him, after Solano broke it off, she had gone off the edge. She'd threatened Solano, that last day in his office. She'd told him she'd been keeping notes, and she was going to write her story. Angie was going to expose the business: how there was nothing behind the company, nothing at all. And Whitaker would be her main source.

Rose had discouraged her. It's not worth it, he had told her. *You are angry, you are jealous, and in the end you will only hurt yourself.* She had listened, he thought. She had dropped the idea.

But now she was dead. And Whitaker was missing.

Rose went around to the front of the house. The street was empty. He contemplated waiting, hanging out on the porch. He was pretty deep in the Mission District, though, and the emptiness made him wary. There were a lot of bohemians living here now, his friends had told him: old Beats, people from the mime troupe, revolutionaries from Latin America. But you wouldn't guess by looking. A remodeling project across the street—maybe you could call it gentrification—seemed to have stalled. The site was abandoned, the job sealed in plastic. In reality, a lot of the old neighborhood people resented the newcomers. Maybe it wasn't fair, but he knew their reasons. Two years ago nobody who had any choice wanted to live here. The lesbians had their enclave on Valencia Street, but in this part of the barrio it was poor families and *cholo* gangs and Filipino boys, back alleys full of crack vials and doorways that smelled of vomit. Then came the boom and suddenly a million somebodies were here. Kids from Spokane and Atlanta and Kansas City. From Los Angeles and Baltimore. They had dot-com jobs, or some of them did anyway, and those who didn't were living off money from back home, from parents puzzled about how it cost their kids so much to live tripled up in studio apartments in the worst part of town.

And it was not just the rents that had gone up. The ratty sofa in the used furniture store down on Mission Street was suddenly worth eight hundred bucks. Four hundred for those old motel curtains. One-fifty for the rod to hang them on.

The rickety bar stools and plastic bus station chairs in the junk stores were articles of fashion, spray-painted, decoupaged, patched up with duct tape and glue.

Objets d'art. Objets du style.

And the newcomers decorated up their windows with the Virgin of Guadalupe, and put on their berets. And they walked up Valencia Street, hand in hand, tongue in mouth. Man with man. Woman with woman.

Suddenly he was disgusted with this whole place. With himself. With everything.

He started back toward Twenty-fourth.

I'll walk up to Noe Valley, he thought. I'll catch a taxi. I'll go to the airport and leave this world behind.

It was pure impulse, but why not? It was impulse that had brought him here, after all, and he might as well leave the same way. Meanwhile, he had twenty thousand in the bank. Saved over six months.

Not a fortune. But something.

He had his clothes with him. His laptop. The job down in the South Bay was over, and all of the sudden he was in the middle of something ugly, he wasn't sure what exactly, only that he didn't want to be in the middle anymore.

Rose turned the corner and to his surprise there was a taxi parked in front of the taquería. The driver had purple hair, and on top of the vehicle was an advertisement for *Red Herring* magazine. About to go belly-up, Rose had heard, like the technology market it covered.

"The airport," Rose said, though there was a quaver in his voice. Second thoughts, maybe.

"Climb in. I'll just be a minute," the driver said. "I was just going to grab something inside."

The driver went into the taquería, and Rose climbed into the taxi. He closed his eyes, imagining for a moment the ground far below him, the plane ascending through the fog, the land of gold growing smaller beneath him, far away. He didn't want to be a queen in the land of queens. Living alone in some apartment out in the Lower Haight. It was better to go home, to throw your cards out on the table. But he knew he couldn't do this either. He would go back to the way he had been, folded inside, focusing on his computer in his apartment all alone, the occasional girlfriend, the occasional rendezvous with someone he found more alluring.

Then he glanced down Twenty-fourth at the wash of color, at the palms dipping into the blue light, at a woman swinging her mulatto ass, at the Latino boys lounging up and down—and he knew he'd been hooked.

No, he thought, I can't go back.

He would go to his friend's house. He would leave a note on their porch and come back later. Maybe have lunch in this taquería, check out the stores. Through the window, he could see the driver was still in line. He got out of the taxi and walked around the corner. Halfway down the block, there was the blue van again. A woman leaned from the passenger window.

"Hey," she said.

There she was again, the woman in ringlets. Then the side door slid open and a man jumped out.

"Hey, Jimmy," he said.

Jimmy backed away.

"Let's go for a drink."

Just around the corner there was Twenty-fourth Street, and the taquería, and the taxi, and the driver with the blue hair. There was the woman with the mulatto ass and hombres leaning against the Aztec Grocery. But the man in front of him blocked his way. Rose remembered him now. Max. He held a gun. The woman, though . . .

"Get in the van," said Max.

Jimmy knew better. He took a step backward, and raised his hands. If he got in the van, he would never get out. His intention was to turn and run.

Silvia, he remembered. That was her name. From Tosca's. And the driver . . .

Max fired then. Jimmy fell back. He fell against the wall. Jimmy thought of the taxi, maybe, of the airplane. Of his other self way up there in the airplane, the self that had escaped and looked down at poor Jimmy on the sidewalk. Meanwhile, Max leaned over. The woman in the ringlets was calling out from the van. Max didn't seem to hear. He took Jim's backpack, his wallet, stripping him of his identification. He gave a Jimmy a little pat. Then he fired again.

TWENTY-TWO

The next day, when Dante returned to San Francisco, he didn't have a chance to seek out Marilyn, even if he had been so inclined. He'd thought about it, as he wound his way back through the Sierras—he'd thought of pushing this whole business over and disappearing into the pines, down this long lane, into those clouds, another life—but then Cicero had called on his cell. Jake had spent the last day or so out tracking Whitaker's ex-wife, Ann, following her around Tiburon—from the grocery, to her kids' school, back to the condo—but with nothing to show for it, and in the meantime Jim Rose seemed to have bailed. Of more immediate concern, though, was Nick Antonelli. The man did not return his messages, and he wasn't in his office. So Cicero sent Dante to stop, unannounced, at the man's house in San Mateo.

Barbara Antonelli answered the door.

"Just a minute."

She did not let Dante in right away, but asked him to wait on the porch. The screen was open and he could hear her in the next room, shuffling things about. Meanwhile, Nick wasn't here; Dante could see that. The garage door was open, and the BMW was gone. Finally, Barbara came back. They went to the living room, and she sat with her knees together on the big couch.

It was four o'clock in the afternoon, and she had a drink in her hand.

"I was just going though a few things," she said. "You know. Photo albums, old pictures. I couldn't help myself. And there's the memorial service . . ."

Even in her grief, a little drunk, Barbara Antonelli had a voice like silk. Dante remembered it from when he was young. Angie's voice had been rougher—with her father's intonations, the quick starts and sudden stops. Dante remembered listening for the sound of her mother's voice in Angie, for the soft lilt, and being disappointed when it was not there. Then, all of a sudden, he would hear it when he least expected: when she leaned forward to order a glass of wine, maybe; or at night, as she lay beside him in bed.

"Jake asked me to stop by. I haven't been able to get in touch with Nick, and we wanted to give you an update on what we've been doing. I know Nick told us to discontinue the investigation. But he'd paid the retainer, and Jake felt—"

"He asked you to discontinue?"

"Didn't you know?"

"My husband never mentioned anything to me," Barbara said, then she seemed to give it a second thought. "Or if he did, I let it go. It's possible, you know, that Nick told me but I didn't hear. That it slipped away from me—given everything."

From where he sat, Dante could see the swimming pool with the pergola in the background, and the bronze hills, and the embankment that hid the freeway. The curtains were brocaded and there was a hanging lamp in a style of thirty years before, resin and colored glass, that dangled like a balloon over the couch. Barbara wore a polo shirt and a denim skirt, and her eyes were hollow from lack of sleep.

"Angie—" Barbara stopped, as if unable to speak. Then she went on with it. "Her body is still with the city. We have to make some kind of arrangements or the city will bury her. They won't hold her forever."

"Have you scheduled the services?"

"I'm trying to. Day after tomorrow. But Nick . . . You see, the casket's a special order. He had this thing—wood from Abruzzi. Italian oak, I don't know. Meantime, the body's in storage, and he won't sign the release."

"Why don't you sign it?"

"How do you think he'd react if I went down and did that?"

Dante knew how Antonelli could be. Blowing up one minute, then sweet as hell the next. Hot-blooded, volatile. Didn't want anyone taking action other than himself. Though Nick was a sharp businessman, he would vacillate sometimes, swing back and forth, then act all of a sudden, on sheer impulse. It was one of the man's strengths, Dante knew, that impulsiveness, but it also got him into trouble. He was self-assured, a blusterer, but at the same time that glint in his eyes betrayed him—as if there was something dark and secret inside, a reservoir of shame.

"I suppose I should be worried about him," Barbara said.

"It's a hard situation."

"Nick's been on a jag for months. For years really. And now, well. The doctor gave him some tranquilizers, but you can't knock him out. He's like a horse. And meanwhile, he keeps drinking."

As she said this, she took another drink herself.

"From what Jake said, Nick wanted to move on. To accept what happened. He was worried about you—the stress of having things unresolved."

Barbara laughed then. It was a dry laugh.

"That's so very kind of him."

"Yes," Dante said.

Then he went on to explain to her what they had found out, from Rose, about the problems at Solano Enterprises. And he told her about Whitaker's death. She listened with a vague discomfiture.

"It doesn't prove anything, though, does it?"

"There's one other thing," he said.

"Just one?"

"You were out at Angie's place before you took me there?"

"Yes."

"Her laptop," he said. "I know when Angie first met Solano, she was working on a story."

"You asked me about the computer before."

"It just seems odd to me that it would disappear."

Barbara took another sip. It was just ice now and she rattled the cubes in her glass. "I would have told you if I had seen it, wouldn't I?"

"Angie was always writing," he said. "In those old journals of hers. I was just wondering, she probably kept her journal on the computer now. And maybe it would give us something to go on."

She shook her head.

Dante stood up. He went over to the dining room table now. She had been looking through the family photos, and there at the top was an old sepia tone, not of Angie but of Nick. Antonelli stood with his arms folded, a man on either side of him, dressed in the old style, with the old fedoras. It took Dante a minute, but then he realized the photo had been taken on the steps at the church. There were some children off in the background, and it occurred to Dante the photo had been taken the same day as the communion photo.

"Who are these men?"

"I don't know," Barbara said. "Just some old-timers. You know how Nick was. Always schmoozing with everybody."

He put the photo down.

"Do you want us to continue investigating?"

"You better ask my husband."

"Do you know where he is?"

She shrugged—and Dante understood from that shrug. He could be slow on the uptake, but he understood now. Nick was with his mistress.

"I need to talk to him."

Barbara swirled the ice and looked into the glass. She shook her head, walked away. Refilled her glass. She stood with her back to him. He studied the slope of her body. "It's his secretary," she said at last. "She has a place up on Russian Hill. I'll get you the address."

TWENTY-THREE

Eccentric the cat lay on his side in the high grass. His fur had dried, and the skin was pulled back from the teeth. Barbara Antonelli had not yet located the cat, but this did not mean the animal had gone undiscovered. The insects had found him, the blowflies and the nettle bugs, and there had been some rats the night before, and this morning some kids had poked at his corpse with a stick. Then this afternoon the turkey buzzards had come, two fat and ugly and not particularly graceful birds with red wattles and oily skin. They squabbled as they ate and, when they were done, perched in the tree above, eyeing the sky and each other, waiting till they had room in their guts to gorge some more. Meanwhile they shat out their foul shit and peered at the neighborhood. At the houses and the tall grass and the oak. They saw it all through their turkey buzzard eyes. The sun was bright overhead and the sky was white. Once this had been church land, and Spanish padres had walked on this hill, and a rancher's son had gotten lost in this canyon, and the ancestors of these birds had picked at the corpse in the same way these birds picked at the cat. It was still the same deadness in the air, the same sense of nothing at the heart of the things. A hawk circled overhead, then two more buzzards appeared in an adjacent tree. The earlier vultures eyed the newcomers, then swooped down on the carcass with a graceless thud. They had been here first; after all, this was their territory, their feast. Soon all four birds were at it, hopping about, squabbling, tearing the cat apart. Occasionally one or the other would retreat to the tree, with a bit of the flesh hanging from its beak.

Meanwhile Barbara Antonelli stood in her backyard. She saw the birds, and they looked to her like something in a dream. It did not occur to her, not yet, what they were doing. She had already determined, though, that Eccentric was not going to come back. She did not call for him anymore. The cat had been her last connection to her daughter, or almost the last.

She had lied to Dante.

She had found the computer in her daughter's car, in the trunk of the Corolla, in the garage over on Union. She had found it before they'd hired Dante, and started snooping through it idly at first, in the same way she used to snoop in her daughter's dairies.

The journal was a rambling affair. It did not stay on one topic. Dante was right, though. Angie had been taking notes when she'd first met Solano, notes about the man himself, romantic stuff, mixed in with the mundane details of her day, her job, and the growing realization that Solano Enterprises was not what it seemed. At some point in the journal she had brought up her father's association with the business, and the tone was sheer bravado, tongue-in-cheek. *They do not know who they deal with when they deal with Nick Antonelli.* Then she changed subjects, went off on a tangent about this, about that, about the coastline of Catalina. About her mother, Barbara Antonelli, and how she closed her eyes to things she did not want to see. Then the journal changed. Things went sour with Solano, and all the details were there . . . how Angie went off the handle, threatening, meaning what she said but not really . . . trying to hurt back, to scare. Then she had gotten afraid herself. There were people behind Solano, and people behind those people . . . money at stake . . .

Nick knows, Barbara thought.

Angie was murdered, and Nick knows. If he didn't know at first, he knows now, even if he pretends to himself that he doesn't. But he knows. She had seen it in his eyes. He had more to do with it then he was willing to admit.

Still, she hadn't given the journal over to Dante.

You would think, she thought, after all Nick has done, I would have no loyalty left in me. But maybe my loyalty is not to him but to something else. To a world that I imagine for myself, and don't want to abandon. But such loyalty, it doesn't mean you have to forgive.

She dialed Nick now. She left an ugly message on his machine.

Meanwhile, she could see the buzzards in the tree. She stood in her green skirt and her olive blouse under the gold sun. The buzzards were masticating. I am dreaming, she thought, and, in this dream, the next time I see Nick, I will drive a knife into his heart. She looked at the buzzards and suddenly she understood. She understood everything. She was not the dreamer. No. It was the buzzards who were dreaming her.

TWENTY-FOUR

Nick Antonelli was with his mistress, Anne Marie, in the apartment towers atop Russian Hill. Her balcony looked down into The Beach. It was a yellow concrete bunker of a building, very contemporary on the inside, that loomed out over the hillside. Now, standing on the narrow balcony, Nick was filled with vertigo. A few minutes ago, his wife had left a message on his cell, but he had not listened. Meanwhile, Dante Mancuso was looking for him, he knew, and a police detective who'd just been transferred to the case. Nick could see the cop station from here, too, and the square. Perhaps Dante was down there at the moment, wandering about. The cop, too. Sooner or later there would be an intersection. Sooner or later their trajectories would cross, and the crossing would seem like coincidence, or fate, depending upon how you looked at such things.

From his mistress's balcony, Nick could see his daughter's apartment building down below him, at the base of the hill. And he could see Mortuary Row farther on, nestled in the little valley, and the small dark figures on the sidewalk gathered around limousines.

"Why don't you step inside?" Anne Marie said.

Anne Marie was a vital young woman, a brunette, who had come to work at his office about a year before. She had full lips and a slant nose and gray eyes and a smile that wouldn't quit. She was a year or so younger than his daughter, if truth be known, though a different type altogether.

"Come inside, Nick," she said.

Though there was nothing about her voice that any man could object to—throaty, deep, resonating with womanly empathy—she could not comfort him now.

"I'll make you a plate," she said.

Goddamn Solano, he thought. Goddamn La Rocca. Goddamn the whole fucking business.

A long time ago his father had told him. Don't stake everything on one deal. Don't put all your meatballs in one fucking basket. If you do, you'll get desperate. You'll end up with blood on your hands. And his father had known. Because he'd had all his money tied up in the shipping business, and when the workers went on strike, he'd had to bring in the knuckles, as they used to say.

Like father, like son.

His cell rang again. He squinted at the screen. It took someone with tiny hands and perfect eyes to work these things. Small blond girls with slender fingers. Drug dealers with their hats turned backward on their heads. Midgets from Tokyo. No, these cells weren't designed for people like him, middle-aged wops with fingers like fat cigars. Fingers that mushed the keys. Fingers soft and pudgy, like an old man's dick. He felt like hurling the damned thing over the edge. Then the name flashed up. He swore, but it wasn't his wife, at least, or that goddamn Dante Mancuso. It was Gucci, calling from the Diamond Mortuary. Up out of the basement from humping some corpse. They used to joke about him when they were kids, imagining it. Gucci creaming all over Rosa Perrinello down there in the basement. All over Karen Bolinni and the Zlonkowski girl, too, with her little tits and her pigtails. Now the wind gusted up the hill and he pressed the phone to his ear. Gucci's voice was calm and earnest, soothing. He could see down to Mortuary Row, to the black figures moving around on the sidewalk, the cars pulling into the lot. An evening viewing, no doubt.

"Your daughter's vessel. We found one in Las Vegas."

"Vegas?"

"A business associate of mine, a friend really—he is a supplier to the trade. And it happened that they had a model in stock. The Princesss Corombona. Very beautiful. But the price— I wanted to be sure."

"That's not the model."

"It is the previous model. With the ivory princess. It is, if anything, a little nicer—the quality of the wood, cut from an older grove. But the cost—"

"Screw the cost."

"Yes, I know, but—"

"Just get it. I don't want to listen to numbers. I don't want to ever hear a number again."

"Yes. It's very beautiful. Absolutely elegant."

The small black figures in front of the mortuary had clumped together, and their numbers were diminishing. Filing inside the building, disappearing, like ants vanishing into a crack.

"Shall we go ahead with the arrangements," asked Gucci.

"Yes."

"I will need your signature."

Antonelli knew what the man was getting at. He thought again of his daughter's remains up there on the police slab. Of the beautiful wooden coffin. The princess carved in ivory.

Gucci was still talking.

"Hello . . . Mr. Antonelli . . . Our connection . . ."

Nick felt divided. He didn't want to bury his daughter. But he didn't want her on that slab either.

"Shut up," he said.

Gucci fell silent, there in the static. I am trapped, Nick thought, there must be something I can do. He hung up on Gucci and found Anne Marie standing in the balcony door, with her thick, dark hair and her beautiful face. There is always Rome, he thought, I can always cash it in.

"I'm going out for a little while," he said.

"Let me make you something to eat."

"No."

"I don't think it's a good idea for you to go out. You're pretty upset."

"I have some things to take care of."

She tried to embrace him, but he pushed her away. It wasn't much of a push. He'd been rougher with her plenty of times, pulling up her skirt, making out against the wall. Even so, he saw the hurt look on her face, and felt the ugliness on his own. She had set out a plate with prosciutto and cheese, and also a bottle of wine waiting to be poured. He swung his hand and knocked the whole business to the floor.

"I can't do this any longer," he said.

The look she gave him reminded him of his wife, his daughter. A look that had fear in it, love. When he saw such look in a woman's face, he knew he controlled her and could not stand to be around her much longer.

"Go to your wife then."

She didn't mean it. She would take him back at the drop of hat.

"Fine," he said. "I am already gone."

Before Anne Marie, another woman had worked in his office. And before that, another. He had given them good salaries, but Anne Marie more than the rest had nothing to complain about. She had this apartment.

You're a louse, he told himself.

He headed down the hill, toward The Beach. He was headed to Gucci's, to sign the papers, then to the church to give the priest his fatass check, so his daughter could get the burial she deserved. But he couldn't bring himself to do it, not yet. Instead, he walked around the neighborhood, all the old places. What he was looking for, he didn't know. Eventually he found himself at the far end of Columbus, standing in front of Rossini's Bar. His father used to come here, and his father's father before that. From what he understood, one of Rossini's sons, Tony, still ran the place. Tony was close to his own age—one of those who clung to the old ways, who acted like it was 1952 and he was a guy from the neighborhood, with a macaroni up his ass and an accent like he justa step offa da boat. But Tony wasn't behind the bar. It was some kid with a green streak in his hair and an earring dangling down. Antonelli looked around the place. Some kind of Tuesday crowd. Not a person he knew, young or old. He turned to leave, but just then the bartender asked what he would have.

"Dewar's," Nick said. "Dewar's with a beer back."

There were a lot of family pictures on the wall. Rossini this and Rossini that, but it was easy to see that it was all a crock. If you were honest about it all, the neighborhood had been dismantled long ago. Maybe those people on the wall had sweated blood once upon a time, riding their donkeys up and down the street, but it was all bullshit now. Just tourists and Chinese. And these new jackasses in their silk shirts and their cowlick hairdos who expected to make a million bucks jacking off in front of the computer.

"Another round?"

Antonelli pursed his lips and pointed them at the glass. His father had used to do that. The old ones, whenever they wanted anything, they pointed with their lips. Give me this, give me that. I look, I grunt, I want.

The kid seemed to understand.

The television was tuned to the business channel. All stock market, all the time. A ticker tape ran across the bottom of the screen. They were in the midst of a financial catastrophe and the anchorman was excited to beat hell. All the arrows were pointed down. Some kids at the end of the bar were yapping away.

"Time to buy," said one. "It's a buying opportunity."

"Venture's pulling the plug."

"Not on Intel."

"On everyone."

"I don't believe that. Just wait—you don't want to miss the bounce."

The first time Antonelli had ever been to this place he had been maybe five years old. He had sat on his father's knee, and old man Rossini had been behind the bar. The place had been full of those wide-chested Italian men with their white shirts and their oversized slacks, slipping back and forth between Italian and English. Men who spent their days speaking the language of pipe wrenches. Of fishing boats and hammers.

Grab too much and your hands come up bloody.

The kid at the bar looked familiar.

"Who the fuck are you?" asked Nick.

"Jim Rossini."

"Tony's son?"

"Yes."

The kid's chest went out a little. Full of himself. Full of the goddamn world. Tony Rossini had six kids, a half-million grandkids. A wife with a fat ass who got on her knees and gave him a blow job whenever he walked into the room. This kid with the green hair was no doubt one of her progeny.

"Who are you?" the kid asked.

Antonelli hesitated. The people in the old days had respected his father, to his face, but behind his back, they said things. Once upon a time, Nick had wanted nothing more than to be like those men who came to Rossini's Bar, but even those slobs, those carpenters, those fishmongers, they had a chip on their shoulder. But he had shown them. He'd married Barbara Como. He'd made a million bucks.

"My name's Antonelli," he said. "Nick Antonelli."

"Oh. Pleased to meet you." The kid put out his hand, but it was apparent the boy had never heard of him.

"One more?"

Nick went back to take a piss. He scrolled through the cell and dialed up the message his wife had left.

I know what you have done. I know everything.

Her voice was like a cold finger on his heart. *You killed her. You murdered your daughter.* She went on. Something about a computer, a journal that Angie left behind.

He stepped outside.

He wished he could say the streets were full of ghosts. That as he walked down the streets the eyes of his ancestors were on him. That he could feel their presence, and as he walked down to sign over his daughter's corpse, to commit her to burial, he felt himself joining with those who had gone before. But it wasn't true. There were plenty of people on the street, yes. People with sad eyes and drooping lips and shoulders that sagged. They were all around him, yes, but they were not ghosts. There was nothing spectral about them. No, these assholes were all flesh and blood.

Dante had the bolt cutters with him now and he climbed the ladder on Fresno Street. His tenant, Lisa, stood below him in the kitchen, arms folded, watching. Snapping the bolt proved the easy part; the lock gave way without much trouble. Getting into the attic itself proved more difficult. The crawl space was lower than Dante remembered, and he had to wriggle his way through the hatch, angling in, leaving his feet to dangle free a moment as he scootched forward on his stomach. He crawled on his knees now, leaving Lisa behind. It was not an easy entry, but he remembered his mother up and down this ladder, obsessed with her knickknacks, her boxes, her photos.

Pigeons, he thought, or a nest of rats. Maybe that's what was making the noise. Whatever it was, though, it was not the real reason he was here.

Dante shook his head.

Bad as his mother now. There were other things he should be doing.

Seeking out Antonelli. Or Jim Rose. Or just turning this over to pest control and getting back to his life.

Instead he was here again, in the house on Fresno Street. After the dementia set in, they had been been unable to keep his mother out of the attic. Dante had been with SFPD then, as a young detective. He'd stop by, and she would be up here, in the attic, going through boxes. Arranging. Rearranging. Muttering.

The boxes closer to him were neat and well ordered. His mother's handwriting was on the boxes even now. *Nanna. Pappa Pellicano. Dante.* Farther along, things were not so orderly. Odds and ends lay scattered on the joists: statuary and a Christmas crib and the infant Jesus in his swaddling clothes.

Dante pointed the light ahead and crawled along after it. The smell up here was not so good. He could see, toward the rear, that some of the large boxes had been disturbed. They had been knocked over, and clothes were strewn about, and old papers as well. His mother's doing, maybe, all those years ago. Dante went along a little bit more and the odor was more pungent. There was a shaft of daylight in the recesses of the attic, coming through the south wall, and he saw one of the vents had last its grill work. He considered going forward and trying to fix it, but it appeared the flashing was missing. There was another area he could not see, behind some plywood sheathing. Something could be nesting back there, he supposed. He shone his light along the eaves, but the old rattraps were empty. Farther along were torn boxes and yellowed clothing that been slashed and strewn over the joists.

The mess puzzled him.

He retreated now, crawling backward. Near the hatch, he paused to look through the boxes. After a while, he found what he wanted.

A tin cigar box from years ago.

When he came back down, Lisa was standing in the kitchen. She glanced at the box in his hand. It was the real reason he had come. The picture on Barbara Antonelli's table had set him to thinking, and he wanted to look at the picture he'd put inside it years ago. He wanted to see the communion photo before it had been cropped—to look again at himself and Angie, the men in the background, the boy off to the side.

"So?" Lisa asked.

"There's a vent knocked out. Some things have been disturbed, maybe. There's a heavy odor. Possums, maybe," he said. "But I didn't see anything. So the thing to do, I'll get somebody out here to replace the vents—and set some new traps."

"Thank you," she said. "But to be honest, like I said, we haven't heard anything, lately, and Tom and I . . ." She hesitated. "I was wondering. Why don't you live here yourself?"

"It's a bit big for me."

The young woman regarded him a long minute.

"I don't know how to tell you this. My company, now, they're having trouble making payroll," Lisa said. "It's not just us. Pensare—down in the South Bay. Viacom. Broadband—all of them. Things have slowed down."

"What about Tom?"

The girl's face was red now. She had a hard time meeting his eyes.

"It's just, I know we said a few days . . . but I don't when we're going to be able to pay the rent. The day-trading thing . . ."

She shrugged.

"What should I do?"

"I don't know." Dante walked away. Then stopped at the door. "Pay me when you can."

Dante went back to his apartment over Columbus. Apartment, really, was too nice a word. The joint was a flophouse. The walls were thin, and he could hear the Chinese woman talking on the phone down the hall, not to mention the Spanish language television in the tiny apartment next to his own. Across the hall, the young man in 3G lay with his door open and the radio on; meanwhile the punksters were hanging from the window above Dante's own, crying out the lyrics of a song they could not quite remember but nonetheless thought funny as hell. And from outside there was the sound of the traffic, the yelps of the tourists, of the Asian gangs, of the skin shop barkers and tattoo artists. And if you could block all this, there was still the noise of the old radiator, pipes contracting and expanding with heat, an incessant banging in the walls.

Lisa's question was a good one.

Why did he live here?

Dante placed the tin box on his bed and lay down beside it. Now that he had the box, he didn't know if he wanted to open it. He knew what was inside. The goddamn thing was bottomless.

His father. His mother. Himself. His grandfather with his nose that was the father of all noses. Pictures of the whole family, with their pelican beaks. Lined up like birds on the wire.

It was a little world inside that box. The world of the father and the son and the holy ghost. The world of the old house. The little blue report card and the confirmation book and the book markers blessed by the parish priest.

Dante still didn't open the box. It was typical of him, Marilyn might say. He didn't stay, he didn't go. He couldn't embrace what was his, but he could not walk away either.

And so he was held captive.

He walked out for cigarettes, down to the place on the corner. It was cold outside and the sky was black now and the red neon shone in the window. He bought himself a pack of Luckies and a small bottle of Jack.

There were a million ways he could go.

He didn't have to return to the little room up there. He could go see Marilyn. He could go around the corner to the Naked Moon. To the dealers beneath the freeway. He could call up Beatrice at Prospero Realty and sign the house over. Go down to the airport and disappear. But he would not do those things, not yet. There was Antonelli out there somewhere. There was a woman yet to be buried. There was a picture of a little girl inside a box.

At that moment, Nick Antonelli came around the corner onto Vallejo, two blocks away. He stopped and pressed himself against the window at Serafina's. The place was closed, and Stella was not there. Nick hadn't been inside Serafina's for years, but he remembered it well, the red-checkered cloths and the metal chairs, the Chianti bottles dripping with wax. He stumbled a little against the glass. He had gone to Gucci's, he had signed what he needed to sign. He had given the priest a check. Then he had stopped in the Golden Spike, and in Al Capps', and in a couple of other places along the way. Now he was here, dizzy with drink, face smudged against the windows of the Serafina Café. Inside which his father once upon a time had sat with the Chicago gangster La Rocca, in full view of everyone, with little Nick on his lap.

The truth was this.

A few weeks ago, Smith had told him there was trouble at Solano. It was internal trouble, people who had a grudge and were going to take their grudge public. If they did so, it would ruin everything.

Nick had not hesitated.

"I know someone. I'll make a call for you," Nick had said. "I'll put you in touch. Then you handle the rest. All the details. Leave me out of it. I don't want to know who or what. I don't want to know a thing."

Inside the windows he saw all their shadows. There was Stella when she was still beautiful. There was Barbara, his young wife, and Angie in baby shoes clutching her mother's hand. There were his father's friends, back in the shadows. The Mancuso boy in short pants. There they all were, back in 1968, inside of Stella's, big cars parked out front and the future just around the corner.

He picked up the phone again, dialed his wife.

"Yes?" Her voice was cold, indifferent.

"It's me."

She said nothing, but he could imagine her in their house on the San Mateo hillside, sitting on the white couch, legs crossed, her face turned to the side, unapproachable as ever, in her sleeveless blouse, her slacks.

"Forgive me."

She didn't say anything.

"I'm sorry," he said. "It's my fault."

If she heard him, she didn't respond. He could hear the sound of the wire, but if she was still there, if she heard him, if anyone was listening, he could not tell.

TWENTY-FIVE

The Pacific Stock Exchange was on Pine Street, in a gray building with stately columns. The old trading floor inside, like the one in Los Angeles, had been shut down. It was gone now, but it was not gone. The floor where the traders had shouted out their bids, working the spread—that physical place was no longer inside the big building. The flashing board with the million numbers was gone. But it was not gone. It was in a million desks in a million houses, ten million. But it was nowhere. In the old days the brokers would come down here early in the morning, to be in tune with that other board in New York, and stand in the hurly-burly of the floor until the trading day was over. Now the board never shut down. The people who had worked the spread and arranged the trades down in the pit were no longer confined to the pit. They were here, but they were not here. Information flowed down the network. It came in fits and starts. Enron has signed a new deal. Qualcomm has split. Oil is up. The pope is dying, and the flu is loose in Beijing. The numbers rose, they fell. A new boom. New rules. Everyone will be rich. The market has its own logic, its own genius, infallible, the network subject to its own rules, sudden blocks, surges, mysterious delays, orders withheld, then suddenly placed—and behind it the mysterious force that moved it all.

Impulses in the system. Synapses. The echoes of which showed up on TV screens while in the gym. In the little handheld devices. On computer screens.

Broadcast through satellite and transformed into voice. Echoed in car radios. On CNN. In prerecorded voices that read bank statements over the telephone.

In the little voice that greeted you in a whisper, first thing in the morning, as your feet touched the carpet.

Give me more.

It was a voice you could hear all over the city, but suddenly it was in a panic. The market was on a slide.

TWENTY-SIX

The next morning, Dante went first to Antonelli's office. It was just around the corner from Serafina's, not far from Mollini's butcher shop. This part of the neighborhood in here, the Italians had used to call Little City, full of greengrocers and tradespeople. Antonelli's office was a five-story building his father had bought in the early sixties, Dante knew, and which Antonelli had sold during the Hong Kong boom—but not without first securing a long-term lease for himself to the top floor. There was a Chinese greengrocer in the ground floor these days, and some T-shirt shops, and upstairs was an herbalist and podiatrist and also a travel agency of questionable legality.

Dante had gone home yesterday and spent the evening going through his cigar box, looking at the old photos. He recognized some of the people in the background of the communion photo, but not all; the old ones at Serafina's could help, but Serafina's was not open yet. In the meantime, he wanted to find Antonelli.

Antonelli's office door was locked, and there was no answer. The window at the end of hall was open. Dante considered the fire escape. Antonelli's office was a couple of windows down, with a narrow iron balcony overlooking the street, but its escape ladder was up. He could probably get there, working balcony to balcony, but he didn't want to get caught for breaking and entering.

Instead, Dante knocked again, and listened. When no one came, he headed out to see if he could find the secretary at home.

Barbara Antonelli had given him the woman's address. Dante didn't guess this was information Nick had passed along to his wife. More likely Barbara had found it on her own. Dante imagined Barbara out here, following her husband, watching from her car as Nick and his mistress walked up the flagstone path. He couldn't help but wonder if perhaps there was something else going on, something obvious he had missed. Barbara had put up with her husband a long time, and though she appeared resigned, jealousy had a way of weighing on you.

He pushed the button. There was a delay, but after a minute or two he heard a woman's voice over the system. It was a husky voice, a bit weary.

"Anne Marie?"

"Yes."

"My name is Dante Mancuso. I'm a friend of the Antonellis. A family friend."

There was a pause.

"Nick's friend?"

"Yes. It's important that I talk to you."

He heard her sigh then.

"What's this about?"

"It's about Nick. We can talk in the lobby. Or outside on the benches—if you would be more comfortable there."

"Is he all right?"

"I think it would be better if we talked face-to-face."

She didn't say anything else, but he saw the response light go dead, and in a little while she showed up in the lobby, on the other side of the glass door. Her lips turned in a wry grimace at the sight of him, worried about Antonelli, maybe, but skeptical of the man in front of her. It was easy to see she hadn't slept, and her beauty had been rubbed raw by a hard night.

She walked with him out to the bench.

"So you're a friend of the family?"

"Yes," he told her. "But I'm also a private investigator. The Antonellis hired my firm about a week back."

"I thought you guys hung around in bedrooms with video cameras."

"Not during working hours."

Anne Marie did not laugh. "Listen, if Barbara's looking to get something over on Nick, that doesn't make any sense. She's the one who's fighting the divorce."

She looked away then, as if she knew the dubious nature of what she had just said. As if she knew Nick had no intention of getting a divorce.

"This has nothing to do with that."

"Who hired you?"

"Antonelli did."

She stared. "That asshole. He doesn't trust anyone. Is he spying on me?"

"No. I'm looking into his daughter's death."

She lowered her head, and Dante could see a little bit of a tremble in the lip. He studied her more closely. She was dressed simply at the moment, cotton shirt, slacks. Either way, he could see she was a good-looking woman—with a certain intelligence in her eyes—and he could understand Antonelli's attraction to her.

"What do you want?"

"Basically, I'm trying to find Antonelli."

"I thought he hired you."

"He did. But he hasn't been returning my calls. And his wife—She said you might know where he is."

"Why should I know that?"

"His daughter is dead. And another man as well, up in Tahoe. So I have some concerns for Mr. Antonelli's safety."

Anne Marie pushed out her lip. It was a big lip. There were tears in her eyes, and he could see that she was fond of Antonelli, that she didn't want to let him go.

"When was the last time you saw him?"

"Last night. But he didn't stay long. He was upset about his daughter . . ."

"Do you know where he went?"

She shook her head.

He pressed for a little while—on Solano Enterprises, on the Waterhouse Building—but she didn't tell him anything he didn't already know. Another thing occurred to him.

"Could he have gone back to his wife?" he asked.

"How would I know?" she all but shouted, and Dante saw the same thought had occurred to her as well. "Sometimes he sleeps at the office. He's done that before, once, when we had a fight. There's a daybed."

"I went there earlier. I knocked, but no one answered."

"Maybe he ignored you," she said. "He likes to do that sometimes. To lie there and brood." She was quiet a moment, then she swore. "Fuck," she said. "I told myself this wasn't going to happen. That I wasn't going to go to bed with that son of a bitch. But I did, and now this happened, and now I'm out of my fucking job."

"He fired you?"

"No, but I know his history. He always goes back to his wife. Then he finds someone else."

"Do you have a key?"

"To his office? I can't give you that."

"I have to see if he's all right."

Dante could see in her eyes what she was going to say next. That she couldn't help herself, even though it made her look desperate.

"I want to go with you," she said.

Dante looked away. He thought of Marilyn. He thought of the life he never got around to living.

"No," he said. "I don't think that's a good idea."

TWENTY-SEVEN

Earlier that morning, Nick Antonelli had heard the knock on his office door. He had lain there on the office couch until he heard the elevator engage, and then he had gone to the window and looked into the street. It was five stories down. Directly below him was a Chinese sundry shop that specialized in herbal medicines. In the morning there was a lot of in and out, old ones coming for their tonic, mothers with their colicky kids. Once, as he leaned out the window, a pen had slipped from his pocket and nearly hit someone below. Alongside the sundry shop was the entrance to the lobby, and Antonelli had studied that entrance this morning to see if he could catch a glimpse of his visitor departing the building.

Dante Mancuso.

Nick had stepped back into the shadows and watched as Mancuso crossed the street. Mancuso had lingered a moment across the way, glancing back to study the building. Then he'd turned the corner at Mollini's and disappeared.

Now Nick lingered at the window, studying The Beach. The

hill was a wash of color. He remembered running in the alleys when he was a kid, conscious of his father up here in his office.

"It's all about land," his father had told him. "All about land. Once you own a piece, never let it go."

Nick had gone along with that dictum, more or less. But the old man hadn't been into leveraging. Nick was different. He'd run a lien against the Weber apartments to buy a building in Cow Hollow, then knocked that into subunits. Made a deal with some Hong Kongers back in the eighties, dealing the building in which he now stood, but securing a ninety-nine-year lease on the top floor, with a graduated rent tied to the Libor. Taken equity out of the old waterfront property. Always extending, leveraging. That was the rule. He'd used it all to swing the Solano deal. Just another step, another move.

"You will either be the king of the world," his father had said. "Either that, or you will be a ruin."

The office phone rang and he ignored it. Then his cell went off. He looked at the little screen.

Smith.

He let it ring.

He'd made a mistake last night. Sometime, in his drunkenness, stumbling about on the street, he'd called Smith. After he'd called his wife. After she'd left him in the cold, saying nothing, letting him twist. Sometime after that he'd called Smith and uttered the unutterable into the man's answering machine. Wailed and threatened.

A foolish thing to do.

Smith would come after him, he figured. If not now, then eventually. And in the meantime, there was still Dante Mancuso.

Mancuso was a stubborn son of a bitch, he knew. Chances were the cops, with no one pushing, they'd get distracted, lose the trail, but Mancuso would circle around. He would figure everything out.

The man had the tenacity of a paranoid, the inability to let go. The truth was, Dante's whole goddamn family had been that way. He remembered the grandfather, with his fucking hook nose, lying in his boat, whispering to his goddamn fish. And the mother, off the edge, that one.

No, Dante wouldn't let go.

The cell rang again.

Smith.

Nick picked up. There was only so long you could avoid what was coming. Sooner or later you had to answer the call.

"I know how hard this has been on you," said Smith. "I know how much you loved your daughter. And you may not want to hear this now, it may seem insignificant, but I wanted to let you know, to ease your mind, that everything's been squared away."

Smith went on then. All the venture money had been secured. Solano Enterprises would be moved into the building soon, just as planned. The cash flow problems were over, so Nick didn't have to sweat. Smith did not mention Nick's call from the night before. And for some reason, this frightened him more than if it had been the other way.

"The market's down," Antonelli said. "I hear everyone's closing shop."

"Our investors are smarter than that. They know those who ride the tide, who stay the course, will reap the profits down the line."

Antonelli understood. He understood it in a blink, and was surprised he had not understood it earlier. Perhaps he had not wanted to understand. It was the oldest game around. Solano Enterprises was a shell, and Smith was the one who yanked the string. He used the investment money to create the shell, and used the shell to attract more investment money, but the company itself was an illusion, and the money kept draining away. And Solano Enterprises had drawn Nick into the deal, getting him to finance the Waterhouse Building so the game could keep going, filling the offices with people, offering stock options down the line, fattening the cow. But with the rumors, with the crash, it had all started to fall apart. No doubt Smith and his buddies were draining the remaining cash even as they spoke.

Himself, Nick, he had been a pawn. And Solano too, he figured. The real players were the venture firms. They drew in the investors and sucked the gravy. And his daughter, he guessed, had figured it out.

"What I want to do is arrange a meeting. I know you have lots of other things on your mind. But some of our people are in town. They'd like to get together with you. Take a tour of the building."

"My daughter—"

"I know," Smith said. "I'm sorry. Sometimes, a little distraction . . . Isn't that what they say at times like this? Keep yourself engaged with the world."

Antonelli struggled to compose himself. He stepped onto the fire grating. There was Serafina's across the way and there was Stella herself, standing in the open door. I am trapped, he thought. Because if I blow the whistle, I ruin myself. And if I say nothing, Smith can take me down at any time.

"These things have a way of passing," Smith said.

"I can see the police station from here," Antonelli said.

"Excuse me?"

"I can see the patrol officers. I can see the little black-and-white cars."

There was no response.

"I think Mancuso, the detective, knows. He will figure it out. He will piece it all together."

"I don't understand what you're saying."

"You killed my daughter," he said.

"I don't see how you can blame that on us."

"I only thought you were going to scare someone. A little push. I didn't know who—"

"You're imagining things. In your grief."

"I didn't know what kind of a son of a bitch you were."

"Tell me," Smith said, and his voice was suddenly very calm. "How's your wife holding up under this?"

Antonelli heard the tone. He understood the innuendo.

"My wife knows nothing. It's me you want, not her."

"Of course."

"I'll go to the police."

"I don't think that would be wise. In your state. You're very upset. You haven't slept. Things have a logic that isn't really there. I think the best thing, if you could meet with our people."

"What do your people intend to do with me?"

"Don't be silly."

"No."

"I've ruined everything."

"What—"

Antonelli lowered his voice. "Okay."

He glanced to the street. He heard a few strains of music, a swelling voice, then an orchestra, and guessed it was coming from Mollini's shop, where the kids, like their father before them, liked to listen to opera behind the counter. Meanwhile Stella still stood in her doorway, and she had been joined by couple of old-timers, old man Mollini himself, it looked like, and George Marinetti, hobbling over his cane. A Chinese man looked up at him, then away, not seeing. No one saw him except maybe that teenager midstride in the crosswalk, crossing against the light.

"I have another appointment."

"When?"

"Now."

"I think this should take precedence."

"I agree."

"Well, let me tell you where to meet."

"Don't worry."

"What?."

"I'll be right down," said Nick. "I'm on my way."

TWENTY-EIGHT

Dante was headed toward Antonelli's office. Up on the corner of Stockton and Vallejo, Joe Mollini stood in the door of the family butcher shop. Dante had gone to school with the younger brother, and it had been the same back then, always a Mollini in the doorway, and the opera playing inside. Joe Mollini was in his early fifties now. In the window, there was the same sign as always, along with his father's recipes for Sicilian meatballs. In the afternoon, the elder Mollini and Marinetti usually came and sat at the card table inside. They came after they had finished their lunch at Serafina's, Dante knew—though likely that routine would change soon.

Dante would not get past Joe Mollini without talking, he knew this. It was the way things were. You walked past the corner of Stockton and Vallejo, you talked to one of the Mollinis.

"Is it sold?"

"What?" asked Dante.

"Marinetti's. Did your girlfriend sell his place?"

"I don't know."

"Come on. You know everything, a job like yours. Marinetti, he says they have multiple offers."

Joe Mollini was a good-natured guy. Like his father, he took things as they came. He was not reluctant to speak up, though, and you could see from his expression that he had feelings on the issue.

"I don't object to anybody making a commission on a sale," he said. "We all have to eat. But sometimes, you know, Prospero's people push somebody to sell when they don't want. I'm not saying anything about your girlfriend, but George Marinetti, he's friends with my father . . . and it's his daughter behind this."

"If he doesn't want to sell . . . ," Dante said, then he fell silent. He didn't know if he should get into this. Meanwhile, the music inside seemed to have gotten louder. Antonietta Stella, maybe, singing Verdi. The opera where the young woman gets murdered in the monastery.

"He will have no choice," said Joe. "If Marinetti gets the offer now, and he decides not to sell, then he has to pay the commission anyway. You see, he's roped in. And if he sells—if he leaves the neighborhood—what the hell am I supposed to do with my father. If Marinetti goes, my father's going to be in here all day—no friends . . . no nothing . . ."

Mollini was agitated now. A car screeched to a halt just around the corner, someone shouted, but Mollini did not turn his head. The streets here were always full of racket.

"It's no good . . . these old men, to take advantage . . ."

The butcher shop sat on a corner, with windows on either side of the building, and Dante could see traffic had stopped on Vallejo and there was some kind of commotion. There was an unearthly noise, a high wailing cry that at first Dante thought came from the music inside, from Antonietta, the famous soprano. Only the noise was nothing like Verdi.

Dante broke away. He was quick, but by the time he got there the crowd was already three deep in front of the sundry shop and growing thicker. The wailing was more ungodly up close and did not sound human. A Chinese woman was on her knees and pulling at her hair and she began suddenly to pound her head against the brick building. A baby stroller lay sideways and a man's body was skewed across it. A small form lay on the concrete nearby.

A doll, Dante thought.

Stella swooned in the middle of the street, head between her knees. Meanwhile Marinetti was wobbling on his cane at the curb, and Mollini's father, Ernesto, was trying to keep him from toppling. A cop from Columbus Station was running down on foot. A Chinese teenager waved her hands, pointing to the balcony overhead, to the stroller. Dante saw them but he did not see them. He was trying to restrain the woman. Then he got another glimpse. The doll wore a little blue cap. Only the doll was not a doll, and blood was pooling beneath its head. The man nearby lay with his feet over the stroller, and his cheek against the walk. Dante had not put together what had happened, but he would in a moment. More onlookers had gathered. Witnesses. People gesturing to the balcony, then to the stroller. To the man who lay on the sidewalk. To the hysterical woman who had emerged from the sundry shop at exactly the wrong moment, pushing the stroller, and whom Dante could no longer contain. She broke away. There were more cops now. The crowd thickened. They spoke in English and Italian and Chinese. The noise they made rose up and was lost in the woman's wailing. Even so, in the background, he could still hear the music from Mollini's shop. Dante looked again at the dead man. Nick Antonelli. He lay at Dante's feet with his eyes open and his skull crushed against the walk.

PART THREE

TWENTY-NINE

In the end, it was simply too much. You tried to resist. To avoid those things which seduced you with the sweet logic of your own demise. You hid your cigarettes in the filing cabinet, you walked a circle around the liquor store, you stayed away from the corner where the sweetest of dreams were sold in aluminum wrapping.

But you could not stay away forever.

Because these things, they conveyed a logic of their own. The logic was powerful. It was the logic of the moment. The logic of no tomorrow. It was the logic that said rot and decay were their own kind of beauty. And the hunger you felt—in your heart, in your gut—it was the hunger for that beauty.

After Dante left the scene on the sidewalk, he started walking. Aimless walking, at least at first, without a conscious destination. He was thinking of the stained nightgown, the missing computer, the mess Barbara had cleaned up from Angie's floor. He was in SoMa, headed toward Brannan, and he saw the underpass ahead.

Suicide, the cops were saying.

He'd heard the talk at the scene, and did not doubt the determination. Antonelli was depressed over his daughter's death and had thrown himself from the window. Dante stood beneath the underpass now. There were some kids in the alley. Homeless, in sleeping bags. Ex-cons crouched around a fire. Meanwhile the dealer was watching. Waiting.

There was foil on the ground. He picked it up. There is something I am not seeing, he thought, something I am missing.

He felt the hollowness inside. It was a void, like oblivion itself, and he put the old foil to his nose now and closed his eyes, trying to remember Angie's face. He looked at the dealer. The man was smiling. The man was coming toward him now. Dante dropped the foil.

He turned and left.

He'd resisted one temptation, but he could not resist them all. Back in North Beach, he went into Gino's place on Broadway, on the old Barbary Coast, and started to drink.

The next day, when he felt the weakness in his knees, and the darkness in his head, and the girl's tongue in his mouth, Dante would ask himself how he had let things come to this. How come he had not figured things out a little sooner, before he'd raised the glass to his lips. Maybe it was the grief. Or maybe it was just because the woman was beautiful and he had been drinking. Maybe it was that the part of his brain that recognized danger had shut down, as sometimes happens when people suspect that they themselves are somehow culpable, and so close their eyes to the punishment they have coming. At any rate, Dante was sitting in Tosca's when the woman came in. It was just after five, and the crowd had started to pick up. On the television the Giants were involved in an early spring rout of the Padres—a mechanical thrashing in which no one seemed to take any real pleasure. The Giants' players were bigger and faster, and their pitcher bullied the ball across the plate.

Dante had gotten a glimpse of the young woman when she first walked in. She had dark hair and a white blouse and by the looks of her worked somewhere in the downtown district. She lingered at the end of the bar—as if waiting to meet someone, perhaps, or wondering if this was indeed the place she had been searching for. In a little while, she stood next to him, trying to get the bartender's attention. By this time the bartender had moved away and was occupied at the well.

"Are you from the neighborhood?" she asked.

She was maybe ten years younger than himself. Her blouse was silk and her hair was up off her face. It was brown hair, longish, pulled up, but with a thin ringlet curling down either side of her cheeks.

"From the neighborhood, yes, I can see."

"What makes you say that?" he asked.

"The way you hold yourself. Standing there."

"There is no neighborhood."

"That proves it then."

"What?"

"That you're from the neighborhood. The rest of us—we wouldn't know. We'd think it was the real thing."

"I guess you've got it nailed."

"I guess I do."

She smiled then, and he couldn't help it, he smiled back. She had something about her, this stranger. A dark-eyed young woman with wide, thin lips that had a kind of wry twist—a Bess Myerson, all-American kind of look that made you feel like you were at a football game with the queen of the parade: the girl with the rich father and the big house at the end of the block.

Twenty-seven years old. White blouse and pencil skirt and a scarf suggestively draped about the neck. Cashmere pout.

"Yourself?" he asked.

"I've been here maybe a year."

"What brought you?"

"Same thing that brought everyone else. What's your business?"

"I used to be a cop," he said, wary, watching to see the effect it had on her. None, it seemed. "Now I am in the private sector."

"Detective?"

He gave the slightest nod.

"I'm a lawyer. Corporate. Used to be in the criminal end—but you know . . ." She shook her hair loose and something in the motion told him she was lying. In the first place, she wasn't old enough. Then she changed all of a sudden, and her voice went soft. "Really, I'm just an assistant," she said. "I haven't passed the bar. I got out of school a year ago, and I spent a year as an intern, in the DA's office."

Maybe that was what disarmed him, that small maneuver—that seeming bit of honesty. Or maybe it was the small crescent of freckles on her cheek. Or the angle of her jaw, how he could see that underneath her well-chosen clothes, she was rangy and thin, and looked more like a kid than a woman.

"Why did you come here?"

"The pot of gold." She laughed. "There's been a lot of hiring, and Westin Financial, they hired me. Internet litigation."

"I heard there was a lull."

"Not for us," she said. "Let me buy you a drink."

She went away to corner the bartender, and Dante stayed where he was. This time of day, it wasn't your usual North Beach crowd. Or not the one Dante was used to anyway. It was a look to the future kind of crowd. With hip haircuts and a vision of how things were going to be, ignoring for the moment anything that contradicted that vision. And for a moment Dante wished he were one of them.

The young woman came back and handed him a drink. After a while she reached out and touched his nose.

"May I?" she asked.

She was coy, but he didn't mind. He let her touch his nose. She ran her fingers over the appendage as if she were stroking something of great value. "It's a beautiful nose," she said, and there was a touch of mockery. "I've never seen anything quite like it."

He closed his eyes. He liked it, her fingers on his nose, there in the dark.

"I want to take you home," she said.

He looked back at her now. Her eyes were very dark and her skin was pale and there was something wrong about the way she said it. Something off about her eyes. It was the look of a person who was perpetually hungry, like those people beneath the underpass. He should have noticed sooner.

"All right," he said. "Take me home."

"Drink your drink first," she said. "I know a place we can get something to eat."

They toasted and he drank a little, sipping it partway down. He looked at her again, and things which should have clicked earlier, clicked now.

"What's that you're drinking?" he asked.

"Mai tai."

She gave him the Bess Myerson smile again. Mai tai. The same drink the girl had with Whitaker, first at the casino, then at the little bar across from the boat dock. Coincidence, maybe. But he did not think so. Last time around, she'd been working with two men—at least according to what Rose had told him. He glanced around, but no one matched the descriptions. Maybe Rose had gotten it wrong, he thought. Or maybe the men were waiting outside.

"I'll be back," he said.

"Taking your drink with you?"

"I am going to ask the bartender for a touch of ice."

He went to the restroom and threw the rest of the drink into the sink. He'd drunk maybe half and wondered how much of a dose he'd gotten, or if he'd gotten any dose at all. When he returned to the table, the girl was still alone. He glanced about again, but again no one seemed to be paying them any mind.

"Your ice?"

"I got tired of waiting. So I drank it down. Where is this place?"

"The Mission."

"We can take a taxi."

"I have a car."

"We'll have more fun in a taxi."

"No. My car—you'll like it."

"Okay."

The smartest thing to do was to stay in the bar. Or call Cicero and get him to follow. But Cicero wasn't answering, and working alone had an advantage. Besides, no one at the bar followed when they got up. Out in the street, it was the same thing. Meanwhile the woman was chattering. She wove her arm through his and smiled big. And he began to wonder if he was mistaken. They went up Fresno Street then, and as they walked he felt something like rubber in his knees. It was an odd sensation, accompanied by a giddiness in his head and a blackness underneath, a steel darkness where there was no feeling or thought. Then the giddiness was gone, and they were suddenly farther down the street, entering a parking lot. A small segment of time had just vanished, evaporated into nothing.

"Kiss me," she whispered, or he thought she did.

She was leaning against him. Her smile was bigger than before, and there was that same off-kilter look, the same hunger. He pushed her against the car. And put his hand on her waist and got a glimpse of her red lips, the white teeth, and there was a moment of embrace in which he felt the rubber in his knees again and the darkness swelling up and then he was in the car with her and she had her hand under his belt, and whole pieces of the clock were vanishing. He'd been doped. Like a million gumshoe detectives in a million improbable stories, taken in by a woman from out of nowhere.

Like Bill Whitaker, he figured. And like Angie as well.

And then he was under.

Sylvia kept driving. She glanced at Dante, how he sat with his head slumped against the window. The detective was not bad-looking, and she wouldn't have minded fucking him. Maybe it was his nose, or his dark eyes, but she had enjoyed the way he assessed her: the penetrating glimmer there at the bar when he looked up from his drink, the way his lips twisted like maybe he'd just realized what was up, knew what was in that drink but couldn't walk away because there was something else he needed to know, a secret he had to unlock. She liked the game of it, and would have liked to play longer, in a hotel room, maybe, riding him from above, his hands on her titties, her wet pussy on his face, that big nose up inside her. But that would have meant slipping him the drink later, after sex, then killing him in the hotel room—drowning him in the bathtub, maybe, like she and Arturo had done a couple of months back with that insurance executive in Sacramento. Drawing things out, though, would have been too much of a risk. There had been too many fuckups already.

Sylvia lit a cigarette and continued on down Highway 101, through Pacifica and up toward Devil's Slide. Halfway up the grade, she pulled down a side road into the eucalyptus. It was a gravel road that ended about a hundred yards from the ocean.

Max and Arturo were supposed to be here by now.

She wished they would hurry. She wanted to get this over with. Aside from everything else, she needed a goddamn fix.

The truth was, San Francisco had been one problem after another. It had started that night at Tosca's. There was always a certain amount of come and go, it was true, the element of chance, things you had to make up as you went along. Sylvia liked that element, she had to admit. She liked the improvisation, the wild swing of it, the feeling anything could happen. So when she'd seen Angie emerge from her apartment in that print skirt, she'd followed. Down the street, into Tosca's. She'd called Max and Arturo on her cell, then she'd sidled up next to Angie girl. They'd started to talk, Sylvia playing the new friend, the girl on the town, making up her history on the spot, the way she could sometimes. Then Max had moved in with his big English mouth. My cousin from England, Sylvia had said. Truth was, she wished Max had hung back a bit longer, but Angie seemed to like him. They were flirting it up pretty well.

Then Jimmy Rose showed up. Not part of the deal, not part of the contract. Not at first anyway.

Probably they should have backed off then. Waited and tracked Angie down later, but the rule was, once you're committed, you're committed, and anyway Rose didn't stick around long. So it worked out okay, it seemed: two couples arm in arm, wandering down to the waterfront. Sylvia and Arturo. Angie and Max. And the rest was pretty easy. Angie started to weave a little bit, silly girl, and Sylvia could see she was going black, teetering, eyes still open but not really seeing, talking but not remembering. Angie girl walked up to the edge of the pier, Sylvia guiding her by the hand, sweet-talking, watching the light pool up in the doomed eyes.

"I love this city," Angie said.

Then Sylvia gave Max the nod. Max came up from behind. He gave Angie the big push, but she did not go over. She staggered, and he pushed her again.

It was not a long fall. Angie made the faintest of cries on the way down, childlike and lonesome, then disappeared into the blackness with barely a sound, like a knife into water. Whatever her struggles, whatever the thrashing, it all took place beneath the surface.

Afterward, Arturo sent Sylvia and Max to Angie's apartment. Arturo kept her in the dark as to the scene behind the scene—or maybe he was in the dark himself—all she knew was that their client, whoever it might be, wanted Angie's computer destroyed as well. Only there was no computer. So she and Max had gotten high. Too high. And Sylvia had gotten into one of Angie girl's nighties, there on the bed, and Max had come all over her leg.

But there was no computer.

They didn't tell Arturo this. Everything went according to plan, they said. The job was done. Finished. Time to leave.

The three of them should have cleared out then, as far as Sylvia was concerned. It was what she and Arturo had always done in the past. Arturo, though, had spent a few years in the city when he was a kid, in North Beach. He hadn't any friends back then, only his dog, a little black cocker, and Arturo grew all weepy talking about the dog. He wanted to spend a few days more in San Francisco. On account of the dog, and on account of his lost childhood, but more than that, Sylvia knew: It was the needle. The hotel room had thick curtains, and Arturo liked to pull the curtains and lay there in the dark, thinking about that dog, with that little wet nose that used to nuzzle him when he was a kid.

So they'd lingered in the city, and then there were complications. Because Arturo had gotten another call.

The dead girl's father had a hired a detective, it seemed, and the client needed a last favor. Shake the father up a little. Don't hurt him, not yet, just scare him. Be creative. Then follow the detectives for a few days. Make sure they are off the case.

She hadn't wanted to take it on.

But it had been fun, she had to admit, chasing the cat off the diving board. Watching the fool thing leap. Laughing while it thrashed through the blue water, tried to find its way out of the pool. Clawing at the concrete lip.

And they were almost finished.

Sylvia reached over now and touched Dante's nose. How close he'd been to figuring them out, she didn't know. *Naughty detective.* Either way, she imagined herself with him in that hotel room. She imagined blowing into his ear, sweet nothings, whispering, and him all the while with that look in his eyes like she was the one who could unlock the secret. Who knew the story behind the story. She put one hand on his pants, the other on his nose. She caught a glimmer of steel in the rearview, moving through the trees. *It's too late now.* Then the blue van appeared, pushing a swirl of dust. *You're never going to know.*

Max was driving. This concerned her. It was Arturo's van, his pride and joy, and he never let anyone else drive.

"Where's Arturo?"

"In the back," he said. "Taking a nap."

Sylvia knew what that meant. She looked in Max's eyes and saw the light had gone dim. It had not vanished, of course; it never vanished, but the glint was dull. This maybe was more dangerous, because Max was in some ways even more impulsive when he was high, when all the guardians were asleep and it was just the restless animal inside.

"Is there any dope for me?"

"The man overdid it again," said Max. "The man with the plan. He's useless."

She slid open the van door. It was true: Arturo lay in the bunk and did not look well. Sylvia touched his arm. His skin was not as warm as it should be, and his color was too blue. Meanwhile, Max had gone over to the Polaris and opened the passenger door. He stood there looking down at the detective.

"This guy, I don't see how a woman can stand looking at a face like this."

"What do you mean?"

"A face like that. With that thing in the middle of his face. That's a crime against nature."

"His nose?"

"Nose? That's not a nose. That's a dick. That's a goddamn dick in the middle of his face."

"I think he's kind of cute."

"You would."

Max stomped off, following the path to the cliff edge. She knew how he could be. The thing with Rose, it had not been supposed to go that way. They'd had a plan, a way to take care of him, but Max had gotten edgy and pulled the trigger. She did not want that to happen again.

She reached inside the car and touched the detective. He did not stir, and she told herself this was a good thing. He was out.

Max came back shaking his head. "That's a long way down there. I say we get this done quick," said Max.

"What are you saying?"

"I can't do this alone. He's dead weight."

Sylvia realized what he was implying, and she did not like it. The plan had been simple. She would get Mancuso out here. Then Arturo and Max would lift the man out of the car and throw him over the cliff. Not the most elegant of plans, but it got rid of the body, and did so according to Arturo's rules. No gunplay. Nothing to trace. And it looked like an accident. Guy went hiking, fell off the cliff.

"We don't want to get reckless," she said.

Max smiled then. "How about I do it the simple way. Shoot him where he sits," he said. "Right there in the Polaris." Max put on the London accent, doing the James Bond bit. Suave, tongue in cheek. Only Max was no James Bond. "They'll trace the registration," she said.

"Don't tell me you got it under your real name."

She shook her head. "There's no sense in taking any chances," she told him. "Come on. Let's get loose. You leave the gun up at the van. Then we can do this, just like we planned."

"I don't need any," he said. "I'm perfect."

"Good for you."

They went back to the van and unfurled the foil, and in the end Max couldn't resist. She saw his dullness grow a little duller, and then he started to paw her like he had the night at Angie's apartment. Sylvia stopped his hand. "Get rid of the gun," she said. Truth was, she didn't mind it, the gun there in his pocket; she didn't mind touching the gun while Max touched her, but if she had any say with him, she had it now. Meanwhile Arturo still lay in the bunk, and she could see his foot hanging over. The way it hung there, it was not a normal-looking foot. Poor Arturo, she thought. Poor Arturo, who had been like a father to her. Poor Arturo, who had grieved over the beloved wife who used to measure out his dope in careful spoonfuls. Poor Arturo, who had dreamed just this morning of a little dog, chasing him down his boyhood streets, but whose foot at the moment hung over the edge of the bunk, a sad foot, a stiff foot, that didn't have anything left to say.

Meanwhile, Max had her skirt up, the same as the nightgown that night at Angie's apartment. Max could not get hard enough to penetrate her and so he was rubbing himself against her leg. He had put aside the gun, like she asked, and it lay on the floor of the van. While he struggled, she reached out and touched the barrel. It was beautiful, Sylvia thought, and for an instant she imagined there might be a whole new way. It was her and Max now. Her and Max and the gun. But she did not trust Max and they would do it Arturo's way tonight. For old time's sake. Then Max came all over her black skirt. The light in his eyes was gone. Arturo's dead foot dangled overhead.

"Come on," she said. "Let's finish our work."

They went over to the Polaris and she saw a vague flicker cross the detective's face, the eyes fluttering.

"Grab his feet," said Max. "I'll take the head."

"I don't think he's all the way under. I think he's coming to."

"How can that be?"

Max grabbed the man by the nose. The detective opened his eyes, but it was just reflex. His head lolled and his eyes crossed. Max turned the nose again a little harder, just to watch the eyes cross again—as if the man were a tweak doll on a kid's bookshelf.

"What are you doing that for?" Sylvia demanded.

"What do you propose I do?"

She crouched on her knees and looked up into Dante's face. "He's in a transitional state."

"What does that mean?"

"It means we do with him how we did with the girl on the boardwalk. Coax him out, tell him we're going for a little walk."

Max stood straight up. He glanced back at the van, then at the ocean. He was dubious, she could tell, and Sylvia herself had a moment of doubt. Maybe Max had the right idea: Just shoot the guy and throw him in the ocean. But then Max shrugged and leaned into the car.

"Come on, dickface," he said. "We're going for a little stroll."

Dante had never gone fully under, but was in and out of consciousness. Partly, it was how the drug worked. It took away short-term memory. Dante did not remember the drive over, even though he had been conscious at times, eyes open. The images simply disappeared from memory as soon as they were registered. But when he saw the girl now, in front of him, he remembered the parking lot. He remembered kissing her. He remembered her lips. Now she helped him out of the car, entreating him to put his arm over her shoulders. There was someone on the other side of him as well. A man, he realized, but he did not remember the man. Then his brain went empty, and Dante experienced the immediate moment again, isolated from the moment before, with no memory of it. He saw the girl's face again, and felt the man's fetid breath, and was aware of his own weight sagging between them as his feet searched for the ground. But the moment was isolated from the moment before, and isolated from the moment after, each an impression in its own right but without connection one to the other.

Dante would have stayed in this state longer, perhaps, except that physical motion tended to wake the brain, and with each step forward the moments connected a little more.

"Thattaboy, prick nose," the man said. "Now you're getting the idea."

"Where we going?" Dante asked.

Or tried to ask. His tongue was thick in his mouth and the words were not decipherable—and anyway he forgot the question as soon as it was spoken.

"Come on, Loverboy. Just around the bend here, you can take it easy."

"That's right," said the girl. "Just a little ways."

Dante watched his feet. He tried to move them more deliberately, and soon he and the girl and the man moved more efficiently, less like a clumsy entry in a three-legged race. "Good, honey," the young woman said. "Very good." They were on a path, and it was narrowing, and then Dante heard a sound that had been in the background all along, though he only now recognized it. The ocean, he thought, and in that instant he remembered Tosca's. The girl in the bar. The drink.

He let his feet go slack. His body sagged, and the trio pitched around violently for a moment, almost tumbling, and in that moment he must have gone black once more. Then the girl stood in front of him, holding his hand, peering into his face. She reached out and touched his cheek.

"It's okay," she said. "We just have a little farther to go."

"Stop that."

"What are you talking about?"

"Get your hands off his goddamn nose."

"You jealous?"

"Why don't you jack him off while you're at it."

Dante's clarity was back. Or he thought it was. He could see the ocean now. The man was somewhere behind him, not far, and the girl was just ahead, leading him by the hand. She turned every once in a while to look him in the eyes, to keep him on track. She smiled with that smile of hers that twisted up at the corners, a girl's smile, and he saw again the odd beauty in her crooked eyes, and behind her the ocean, and all that infinite space.

"Here," she said.

He heard the man behind him, and at the same time heard an inner wheel turning, the secret part of the brain that calculated when you did not know it was calculating, that grasped what was happening at the edge of your senses. They were positioning him. The edge of the cliff was just ahead, and soon the girl would step away, and the man would push him from behind. The drug had taken away the part of the brain that felt fear—it had stripped away all the outer edges, and all of a sudden he had a moment of clarity of the type you can have only when there is no present, and no past, and you are standing on the edge of the cliff with nothing but sky in front of you.

The girl's eyes coaxed him. She pulled him by the fingers, lightly, her body cantilevered toward the sea. She was going to step away now, this moment, now, leaving him on the cliff edge, tottering, on the verge. And in that instant he did a simple thing. He took ahold of her wrist. She pulled in the opposite direction, an instinctive reaction, trying to break his grip. The man grabbed Dante by the shoulders, trying to yank him away. Dante let go. The girl hovered for a moment, one foot in the air, mouth open.

"Oh," she said.

Then she was gone, over the edge. Clawing at the air.

The two men, carried by momentum, tumbled backward. Dante

had had training. The dark calm that had settled in his brain was gone, shattered by adrenaline, and his movements were automatic, brutal. He drove his elbow into the man's temple, then a knife hand into his throat. He picked up a rock and smashed it into his face. He smashed the rock into the man's mouth and then lifted it again, and smashed into his eyes, into his nose, and then smashed him again. He could not stop himself. He smashed the man's face until it was a pulp. Until the skull cracked and the face was raw with blood. Then he stood up and looked down into the cove.

Sylvia lay some hundred feet below. She lay there in her white blouse and her pencil skirt and her black boots, her body sprawled and broken. She lay on a rock shelf with the line of the surf maybe ten feet away and the tide rushing in.

Dante backed away. He meant to find the path but instead tripped over the Englishman's corpse and stumbled along the clifftop. A few steps more and he collapsed into the weeds and the succulents growing helter-skelter along the rim.

This time Dante didn't get up. He put his face into the sand and let the darkness come.

When he woke, it was night. There was an offshore breeze and the sky was clear and there was a moon overhead.

He walked to the edge. The tide had come in, and the waves were up against the cliff. It was a small cove, with a rock reef at the mouth, and the water churned violently. Just because the tide had come in, though, didn't mean the girl's body had been taken out to sea. Dante knew this from experience, from seeing bodies of people who had drowned in coves like this. There were eddies and cross-currents, whirlpools within whirlpools, and it was not unusual for a corpse to be buffeted back and forth, smashed over and over against the rocks.

Dante went back to the Englishman. He was tempted to leave the son of a bitch where he lay, but there would be forensic evidence, he knew, small details connecting him to the death, and he might as well put those to a minimum. Dante rifled the man's wallet first, pulling the identification. Then he grabbed him by the ankles and dragged him to the edge of the cliff. The next part was not easy. He propped the man on the edge, into the sitting position. Then pushed him over. The cliff was sheer, jutting over the inlet, and the man hit the water more or less in the same spot where the girl had landed hours ago, before the tide came in.

Then Dante walked over to the van.

Inside he found the corpse of Arturo Lind. He searched the man's wallet, and found the gun, too, lying on the floor. Then he returned to the corpse and unbuttoned the shirt. It was not easy to get it off, and the shirt stank of death, but he had no choice: His own shirt was covered with blood and he could not be wearing it in public. Then he drove the van toward the edge of the cliff, creeping along the path, until he was in the spot where the Englishman had gone over. He released the emergency brake and got behind the van and pushed. There wasn't much of a slope but there was enough. The van went over the cliff and into the ocean.

He drove the girl's Polaris out to the airport and abandoned it in long-term parking, then took a taxi back into town. When he reached his apartment, he left a message for Cicero's people, asking for a check on the VIN numbers and the registrations and the various names he had pulled from the wallets. Then he fell asleep, a sleep that was deep and black, but by no means black enough.

When he woke up, he was still wearing the dead man's shirt.

THIRTY

That afternoon, Barbara Antonelli had visited with Father Campanella. The priest had come to the house to give comfort, and to get material for the eulogies, as it had been years since he'd seen their daughter. After they had talked for a little while, Father Campanella asked Mrs. Antonelli if she wanted to take confession.

"There will be communion tomorrow, and if you would like to go . . ."

Father Campanella was a kind man, by no means a stickler, but he was a priest, nonetheless, and Barbara Antonelli knew what he was implying. She had not taken the sacrament for some time, and it was best, before communion, to unburden the soul.

"No," she said.

She could see the priest's confusion. He leaned forward, concerned, wondering perhaps if she had misinterpreted him. If her grief had muddled her senses.

"I know this is very hard. I think it would be good for you to take communion with the congregation. Self-forgiveness—regarding things beyond your control—but if you're more comfortable with another confessor . . ."

"No, it's not that."

"I know there's a tendency to blame ourselves, at such times," he said. "And maybe this is what happened with your husband. Maybe that is why . . . What I am trying to say, sometimes one person takes the leap into despair, and another follows, imagining that their sins are so great, there is no forgiveness. But that, too, is a kind of vanity . . ." The priest hesitated. "What I am trying to say: The Lord is kind. Whatever you imagine you have done, let me assure you . . ." Barbara started to sob then. He reached across to her, put this hand on her hand. "Lower your head, please, and close your eyes."

Father Campanella said a prayer. It was a prayer for the living who were left behind, a prayer that entreated her to close her eyes and let go of her sins. It was the prayer for the deaf and the dumb, for the dying, for those paralyzed by deed or emotion, unable to move their tongue: a prayer by which those without speech could simply close their eyes and let loose of their sins, but she did neither of these things.

At the end, Father Campanella waved his hands over her head in the gesture of absolution.

"Tomorrow," he smiled. "Take communion."

But she had let go of nothing. She kept it all held tight.

The next day, at the funeral mass, a moment came when Barbara Antonelli felt herself at the center of attention—as if everyone in the old cathedral were sitting in judgment, waiting to see what she might do. It was a big service—bigger than the church had seen for a while. The Antonellis had roots in the community, but there'd also been a story in the paper: about the daughter who'd drowned and the father who'd jumped to his death, and the ornate caskets coming all the way from Italy. So the place was brimming with people: old Italians she'd assumed dead long ago; North Beach hangers-on; suburbanites, like herself, and their children and grandchildren, too. And the old ones from Serafina's. And Dante as well, sitting in a pew across the way. But there were also people she did not know: fallen Catholics drawn to the ritual, maybe, come to sit in the old cathedral, amidst the chanting and the incense. Come to see the grieving mother and the ornate coffins arranged at the front of the church.

Gucci had done well to procure the coffins, she knew. First, Angela's. Then at the last moment, her husband's, made from the same Italian oak.

Barbara sat in the front row, in the widow's seat. No doubt everyone was watching her. No doubt they had their comments, on how she was dressed, on how she held her head. No doubt there were those who speculated that there was something else behind the deaths—and those who wondered why Father Campanella had agreed to a church service, given her husband's death was a suicide. But Nick was from the neighborhood, and on more than one occasion, he had given grandiose sums to the church.

After the opening liturgy, Father Campanella took the pulpit. He talked about a moment many years ago when he had seen father and daughter at the church, and how he'd noticed then a certain light in their eyes, a light that was similar in its exuberance, in the way it beheld the world. The priest talked about how everyone who ran across the Antonellis, whether it was the father in his office or the daughter at the newspaper, they immediately found themselves staring up into the light of those dark eyes, swept away by these appetitive, emotional people who wore their hopes and fears on their faces for everyone to see. Barbara Antonelli, as she listened, realized that many of these people in the church had their own memories of Nick and Angie, and it was as if all those different versions of her husband, of her daughter, were here in this room, in her consciousness, and the church itself were a kind of prism, the coffins at its center. The light fell through the stained glass, reflecting from the polished caskets, there at the foot of the altar. Barbara glanced at Dante and remembered a moment some fifteen years ago when she had been watching him come across their living room, thinking: yes, this young man is right for my daughter, dark and passionate, a little too dark, maybe, those eyes of his, but earnest. Then Nick had come from behind and smirked into her ear.

"You want to fuck him?"

It was a crass thing to say, but that was Nick. Maybe Dante had heard, maybe not, but either way, he and Angie had broken up not too much later. Nick was a selfish bastard.

I should have divorced him.

Had she spoken the words aloud? She felt suddenly self-conscious, there in the church, with all those eyes on her. There were the many eyes, and the many minds, and the one mind that lived in the many, the single consciousness that saw her thoughts in their nakedness: that saw her sitting with her daughter's laptop glowing in her darkened bedroom in San Mateo, reading Angie's journal that in the end was only partly concerned with Solano and his crooked business. *I know how my father is . . . I know all the rumors . . . and how he has hurt my mother . . . But the question I have to ask myself . . . Why has she put up with him? Not for him . . . not for me . . . for herself . . .*

Father Campanella lingered at the pulpit, offering his formal remonstrance now, the warning against despair, offering in his stumbling way the same caution he had offered her. The caution against suicide, against the withering of the heart. Because when one of us makes the step into the darkness, another might follow. And we must resist that temptation. Because the world is not a mechanism. The universe is not a random pulse of light. Because we cannot know what was in the Nick Antonelli's heart, or if indeed he did not roll his eyes up to God in the instant before death.

Then Campanella descended from the pulpit and returned to the liturgy. Offering a prayer to the Eucharist. Something about the Light Everlasting. Something about the land of the living and dead conjoined. Something about the blood running down the altar and down the steps of the church and into the square. Barbara knew how the rest of the day would go. She would ride in a black car out to the graveyard, and she would stand with her head bowed, and then the people would embrace her one by one, and one of those people would be Dante, who would look her into the eyes knowing there was sometime she was withholding, but she would not tell him, not now, not ever. Because her daughter had been right. She had an image in her head, and it was too late now to let it go.

Father Campanella raised the chalice. He raised the host. The bells rang three times more. Three times three.

In a moment Campanella would step down from the altar. He would head toward the communion rail with the chalice. She knew what was expected, but she knew, too, that the greatest sacrilege was to take the host when you had not let loose your sins. Because it was true, that night, when her husband had staggered drunk in front of Serafina's, she had wished him dead, wished him in hell, and held a stony silence that let him know she would never let go of that wish, never forgive him, even if she never uttered a word of what she knew, even if she kept up the charade for the world, even if she'd already tossed the computer into the weeds by the side of road, for the weather to destroy, for the buzzards to shit on, because she did not want their laundry hung in public. Father Campanella was headed to the rail now. The congregation was watching, waiting. They would not move until she moved.

She knew what they wanted to see. She went to the altar. She knelt on the marble. Father Campanella waited for her to make the sign of the cross, signifying her acceptance, but this last gesture she did not make. The congregation was gathered around, pressing on either side.

She tilted her head back. He put the host on her tongue. All that was left was the trip to the cemetery, and those empty graves.

Later that day, Dante was crossing through Chinatown when he heard the oompah and the oompah-pah, and the rat-a-tat. The clang-a-bang and the sad horn and the big bass drum. The Green Street Mortuary Band was coming down Stockton, past the Blue Pagoda, and the Chinese Shirt Shop. Past Little City Meats, home of the Sicilian meatball, and Ying's Hopeless Café, with its window display of headless chickens. On they came, with their rickety snares and their kazoos, their sad, sad flutes. The people on the street stopped to watch, and the tourists were delighted, though there were some who did not know the superstition and crossed the path of the parade, looking for a better camera angle. The mourners were Chinese. They carried paper dolls. They carried bamboo toys and peddler drums and pictures of the Buddha Child. At center of the parade were the open cars, reserved for the immediate family, as was the North Beach tradition, and in the last car, alone, rode a woman sundered by grief. Dante didn't recognize the woman at first. Then he saw the placard mounted above the windshield. On the placard was a picture of an infant, all dressed in blue.

THIRTY-ONE

Jake Cicero didn't go much to funerals anymore. It was an endless task, once you committed yourself. True, the living needed you on such occasions; but once you reached a certain age, the burying was endless. So he paid his respects in other ways. He had his girl at the agency send flowers. He signed a card. If it was someone he had known well, he would drink a glass of wine to their memory down at Gino's. And if he could remember, he would send their widow, on Christmas, a gift pack of salami and cheese.

But mostly he didn't think about it too much. The dead were dead, and he was sure they were not thinking about him.

As it happened, the Antonellis' service and Bill Whitaker's were held on the same day. If Cicero was going to go to either of them, it would have made more sense, perhaps, to go to the Antonellis' service over in North Beach. Antonelli had been his client after all, and Cicero had known the family. Instead, Cicero had driven across the bay, and now stood with his head bowed in the back of a little chapel in Tiburon. He had come on account of the Whitaker woman. She wore a navy smock and had a bit too much powder on her face. The little girl was there, too, and the boy, and some members of Ann Whitaker's family. A sister, he guessed. A brother-in-law. Nieces and nephews and maybe a neighbor from down the street.

The corpse had been shipped out to Indiana, to Whitaker's hometown, and so the service here was modest. Cicero stood in the back, and Ann Whitaker glanced at him on her way out. She looked right at him, but her face was pretty much empty of expression.

The last time Cicero had talked to her had been several days back, over the phone, when he'd told her about her ex-husband's death. Her reaction had been muted. She hadn't been inclined to talk to him then, and didn't seem inclined to talk to him now, but he lingered nonetheless, and afterward drove to her condominium.

He brought a tray of lasagna with him that he had picked up from Molinari's deli, and his intention was to carry it up to her door.

He told himself he was here on business, but there wasn't much truth to that. He had gone into her background, done his research, and he doubted Ann Whitaker knew anything about her ex-husband's dealings with Solano, and doubted, too, that there was any connection between her and Angie Antonelli. So he put it down as a courtesy call—tying up loose ends, preserving relationships.

Why am I here?

He knew. Things between him and Louise were slipping. His doing or hers, he didn't know. Probably his. The truth was, Louise had fallen in with that group down at the club, and it wasn't just the cruise she wanted. She had rich tastes. She liked her clothes, she liked her shoes, she liked her restaurants and her languorous dinners. He couldn't blame her. On his part, he liked the way Louise looked when she was dressed to the nines, and he still felt a thrill when she put her hand to her throat and peered at him through those lashes of hers. At the same time, though, being with her, sometimes it was like walking long hours through a shallow lake.

The unhappy truth: between the two of them, himself and Louise, they had left too many people behind. Children. Spouses.

But Ann Whitaker . . .

He picked up the lasagna. Lasagna was a tradition in North Beach. When somebody died, you brought comfort. You stopped by. You brought something to eat, to drink. You talked a little and you did not let the person be alone. You brought lasagna. You brought wine.

She opened the door.

"Yes?"

"I wanted to offer you my condolences."

Ann Whitaker looked at him with his carton of lasagna and his slouched shoulders, and he could see instantly the folly of the whole thing.

"I don't have anything else I can tell you."

"No," he said. "I just came—"

"I saw you at the service. I've told you everything I have to say. I've talked to the police. My husband drowned, and whatever was going on with his business, his life, I don't know. And I don't want to know."

"I came to offer my sympathies."

She pursed her lips. A kid stood behind her, and he saw this woman was not so much perplexed by him as wearied, that there was no condolence that he could give because there was none she wanted, and anyway he was here for his own peculiar reasons. Because he had left two wives behind and a handful of children, and he thought maybe he could get back from her what he had lost. Because he was an old man who wanted to feel young.

She saw all this maybe, but her expression did not change.

"Let me get on with my life," she said.

Cicero stepped away. She shut the door without looking up.

The next day Cicero was in his office. Between the Antonelli case and his obsession with the Whitaker woman, he had let a lot of other things get away from him. Some new cases had come in from the city, from the Public Defender's Office. It was the usual odd assortment. A woman who'd had an anxiety attack and pushed her neighbor down the stairs. A punkster who'd stabbed his girlfriend in front of Wing Piu Projects. A petty thief facing a felony conviction for stealing a stereo. All of these involved knocking on doors, in neighborhoods where people didn't want to see you. All required looking for inconsistencies in the cops' case, things the defense lawyers could use to catch the defendant a break, even if the defendant didn't necessarily deserve a break. Cicero spent the morning looking over the files. Then he put his feet up on the desk and closed his eyes.

Louise was right.

You only had so much time in this world. It was only so long before your heart stammered in your chest, or your breath caught in your lungs. Before your brain turned to jelly and your dick went soft.

He had come home yesterday from Whitaker's funeral and Louise had been out. Out with the girls. Out on the tennis courts. Out to Pedro's by the bay where they could drink margaritas and flirt with the Mexican waiters. When she had come back, still in her tennis skirt, she'd been in high spirits.

I should live, he thought.

We should go on the cruise. We should get the hell out. Me and Louise. But the cruise was months away, and there was the weekend just ahead. Monterey, he thought. I'll make reservations. I'll knock off early and surprise her, and we can beat the traffic the hell out of town.

It was an impulsive thing, but what the hey.

Just as Cicero was about to leave, he got a call from his connection down in records. He had almost forgotten. Dante had left a message the day before, asking him to run a tracer on some names and registrations. Three lowlifes, it turned out, whose names didn't yield much. Sylvia James. Max Bright. Artie Linden, a.k.a. Arturo Lind, with a hundred variations thereof. He turned the name in his head, paused.

It almost clicked, not quite.

Arturo Lind.

What connection these characters had with the Antonelli case, Cicero wasn't sure. Dante had been vague, and Cicero hadn't seen him for days. His gut feeling was the same, there was something else underneath the surface, but Cicero wasn't sure he wanted to know anymore. The girl had drowned and the old man had killed himself, and that was ugly enough.

He called Dante and left what little information he had about Lind and the others on his cell.

He stopped at the Ligurian Bakery on the way, got a loaf, a bottle of wine. As he came up Mason, it occurred to him Louise might not be home, but then he saw her blue Miata out front. A tennis racket lay in the backseat, and a warm-up jacket, but this did not trouble him at the time. It was only later that he thought about how Louise never left her racket in the car. She loved her racket.

He went inside. A pair of sunglasses lay on the counter, and another tennis racket leaned against the stool. A spare, he guessed.

Cicero called her name.

"Louise!"

He was not often home this time of day and did not want to startle her and so he called again. The bedroom was at the rear, and he heard someone moving back there. Louise was changing her clothes, he guessed. Always a new outfit, this one.

He put his hand on the knob, but it was locked.

Someone hissed on the other side; someone whispered. He thought of all that had happened lately, and his heart hammered in his chest. He thought of all the dead, of all the private investigators he knew whose lives had been invaded. "Louise!" he called again, and just then she opened the door.

Louise was in her tennis skirt and her polo shirt but she didn't have on shoes and her hair was mussed. Behind her, on the bedroom deck, stood Frank Strum. Strum was a decade younger than himself, a probate lawyer, recently divorced. He had on a blue polo and a pair of shorts. His shoes were untied and the tongues were all sloppy and untucked. Strum dodged his glance. It was a second-story deck, with no way off except back through the house.

"We were just talking," she said. "I was showing Frank the view."

"There is no view."

"There's the yard."

"It's a beautiful yard," said Strum.

"There is no view," said Cicero.

Then Cicero left. Maybe Louise had her panties on under that skirt, he thought. Maybe she didn't. He walked down to the corner store and bought himself a pack of Pall Malls. If I had a gun, he thought, I'd go up and shoot them both. But he didn't carry a gun anymore. As he stood there, looking back at the house, the name teased at him again, *Arturo Lind,* but he couldn't quite get it. It's my age, he thought, everything's slipping away. Then Louise came down with Frank Strum, carrying a racket. They climbed into her blue Miata and drove away.

It had been Strum's racket in the car, he realized. He should have figured.

THIRTY-TWO

The day after the Antonellis' funeral, Dante went to Serafina's. Inside, it was the same wine-colored light, and the same tablecloths, and the same pictures under the glass countertop. He had brought the communion photo with him, the original, the one that had been in his mother's attic all these years. Meanwhile, Pesci sat in the corner with his walker, smoking, and Mollini was by the window. Stella stood in the middle of the room, wiping a plate clean with her apron.

She called out to Mollini.

"So, Mr. Butcher: I see you have been abandoned."

"You don't have to yell," he said. "I can hear you fine."

"Where's your buddy? Where's your friend Marinetti?"

"It's open house day," said Mollini. "Open house day, he has other things to do. Marinetti, he has a life. Everything is not about Serafina's Café, you know."

"I don't believe that." Stella smiled, but it was the kind of smile you could not tell what she meant. "I don't believe he has anything else to do."

"He puts on his good suit and his daughter takes him to Palo Alto. To the Olive Garden in the mall."

"She takes him there instead of here?"

"The Olive Garden is good," said Pesci. "They are generous with their soft drinks."

"You should stab me for a soft drink," said Stella. "You should drain my blood and lay me out in Gucci's basement."

"So this means Marinetti has sold the house?" asked Pesci. He emanated cigarette smoke. It was a nasty smell but likely better than the stink he might have emanated otherwise: the stink of an old man who seldom changed his clothes anymore and for the past three nights had slept in his black shirt with the red rose stitched into the collar.

"He has some offers," said Mollini. "But I don't know. I think maybe there is a problem."

Stella went to the kitchen and came back with Mollini's order. She set it down with the flair of a prison guard. "Those new people don't have the money they pretend."

"They're clearing out. That's what I hear," said Pesci.

Stella sneered. "How do you know so much, Mr. Diet Cola? Mr. Pepsi Lite, with a twist of lemon? How do you know anything, an old man like you, who never changes his shirt?"

"I have a cell phone. So I know. I hear things. Yesterday my granddaughter, she calls me from downtown. Granpapa, she tells me, there are rooms full of computers with no one at the terminals. It is a sight to see. People kill themselves, times like these, I told her. People jump out of windows. Just like the old days. First one, then another."

Stella shook her head. "This is all Prospero's fault," she said. "Ever since he started working with the Chinese. Just ask Gucci.

First, his father hires a Chinese undertaker. Now they own his place."

"You have a Chinese cook," said Mollini. "He's right back there, cooking the spaghetti."

"Only the noodles. Not the sauce."

"What difference does it make?"

"It makes a big difference. I see people from the old days, they tell me, oh, I should never have left North Beach. So I say to them, I tell them, Come down, I have your picture under the glass. Come down and take a look, I say. But do they come?"

Meanwhile Dante sat at the corner, looking at the communion photo—the old one, the original, before his mother had stripped out the background. It was a group photo, fathers and their children, but also godfathers and uncles. Antonelli stood in the row behind his daughter, and Dante's own father was in the same row, intermingled with a number of other men, cocky as could be. La Rocca and his Chicago boys, Dante guessed, but he did not know who was who. While he studied the photo, he thought about the three people who'd come after him the day before, out on the cliff. Cicero's message had revealed little more than he already knew.

"What is that you have there?" Stella asked.

Dante showed her the picture.

"Your mother was right," Stella said. "The picture is better without them. Who needs those kinds of people in your communion photo?"

"Let me see," said Pesci.

"Nobody to see. Just some Chicago nobodies."

"Oh, Chicago," said Pesci.

Then the old man launched into the story Dante had heard a hundred times. It was a story the old North Beach Italians loved to tell. It proved how they were both tough customers and legitimate Joes. Straight-ahead guys, but also nobody's fool. It was the story of how the Chicago mob had tried to get a foothold in San Francisco. The story changed every time Dante heard it, but the gist was the same. The Chicago mob had sent a couple of their top men down on a scouting expedition, but the North Beach locals had caught word and met them at the station. "Those Chicago boys went back on that same train—but they didn't go first-class," said Pesci. "We sent them freight. And when those meatpackers opened the door to that railroad car, back home in Chicago, well, put it this way . . . That's why we got no mob in San Francisco. That's why Italian North Beach, it's clean as a whistle."

How much truth was in the story, Dante had no idea, but he knew the same old men told other stories. They liked to have it both ways. Sure, they were independent, on-the-level, up-and-up guys, but they knew people, had friends. In Chicago, Italy, New York. And if anyone stepped on their toes, well, just try it, just go ahead and try . . .

Dante handed Pesci the photo.

"Which one is La Rocca?"

Pesci peered. He looked a long time. "This one in the back. And this one over here, that's his son."

Dante glanced over the old man's shoulder. The older La Rocca, standing there in his fedora, would have to be long dead. The younger one would be in his sixties by now. It occurred to him these were the same men he'd seen in the photo at Barbara Antonelli's house, there on the table.

"The son, he moved the business over to Vegas."

"What were they doing in North Beach that day?"

"La Rocca and his family, they came down for the weekend. A

godson was getting his confirmation that day. So they came down, and Antonelli's father, he has a photographer. He likes to show off who he knows."

"I remember La Rocca's godson," said Stella. "He was a problem, that one."

"Maria Mateo's boy. Who was that Polack she married?"

"The priest, he could do nothing. I don't want to tell you what that boy did."

"Which one?" Dante wanted to know.

Pesci put his thumb on the boy who stood at the edge of the frame, the kid just on the verge of motion.

"They sent him off to the country. That boy."

"Lindowski. That was the name. Maria Mateo married him, and they moved out to the Excelsior."

"It was a cocker," said Stella. "A little cocker spaniel. The priest gave it to the boy, a little puppy. And the boy dropped it in a rain barrel and watched it drown."

"Went to work for La Rocca, I remember."

"What did you say his name was?" Dante asked.

"Lindowski," said Pesci. "Arturo Lindowski."

"No, no," said Stella. "It was something else. When the Polack married Maria, he shortened his name. Lind. That was it."

Arturo Lind.

"He was no good," said Stella. "Sick in the head."

Dante understood now. Almost. His guess, from the way she'd been behaving, was that Barbara Antonelli understood, too.

"You see why your mother trimmed those people out," said Stella. "You see why she didn't want them in the picture."

THIRTY-THREE

Down at the Solano Enterprises, there was no longer a receptionist. There was a foosball table still in the lobby, but no one was playing. There were no more croissants on the sideboard, no more muffins, and the latte machine had vanished. Lifted from its place, carried off by a disgruntled employee. In the offices themselves, there stood a number of unattended monitors: computers animated by screen savers—nature scenes, flying toasters, randomizers that broke into color, into city shapes, a shimmering message that read: FUCK YOU, SAN FRANCISCO.

Dante got the feeling the equipment wouldn't be here long. There weren't too many people around, but those who were here, they worked with a fevered, anxious air. In the accounting offices, behind the glass windows, a woman was taking a painting off the wall. Payroll was closed. And in the cubicles themselves, people were stripping their desks, uncabling equipment, carrying it down the hall.

Dante found Solano in his office, standing at the window, looking down Jackson Street toward the Pyramid.

"So you're undergoing a transformation here?"

"You could say that," said Solano.

Solano had pretty much the same demeanor as always, but there was something off. He looked as if something had been dislodged inside him.

"I had an interchange with a couple of your people yesterday," said Dante.

"My people?"

"The same ones who put Angela Antonelli in the bay. Private contractors—is that what you call them?"

"You've got an active imagination."

"So do you, apparently. Whatever you're trying to sell here—it doesn't exist. Angie knew that, didn't she?"

"Existence is a nebulous concept," he said.

It was an odd thing to say, and Dante could see the light gone astray in the man's eyes. Solano's vulnerability, and the fissures beneath the surface, seemed accentuated now, here in the empty building. When he spoke again, though, there was some of the old confidence. "You think about something long enough, you imagine it, after a while it does exist. You bring it into being."

"Angie was keeping a journal," said Dante.

"Our company did nothing unusual. The goal in all of these things is to go public. The goal is to hang in until you have your ideas out of development—and to position yourself. That's the way things work."

"You were afraid she was going to write her story."

"No."

"You arranged it?"

"I don't know what you mean."

"I know your role in all this," Dante said. "I know it precisely. I have Angie's computer."

That last statement was a lie, but Solano did not know that. The man looked over at his desk, as if he wanted something out of the refrigerator underneath. Some crackers and cheese maybe. Imported water.

"When you broke up, she threatened to write her story. You told Smith, didn't you?" Dante said.

Dante didn't have the proof, but it was the only way it could be. Solano had gone to Smith, and Smith had told Antonelli.

So Antonelli had called La Rocca, and La Rocca had hired Arturo Lindowski.

Around the circle, around the horn.

"Antonelli didn't know they were going to go after his daughter," Dante said. "But you knew, didn't you? You knew and you went on your trip out of town—to give yourself an alibi."

Across the way Dante could see the empty offices in the adjoining wing and the randomizers on the computer screens. Bright whirlpools of sand. Of dust. Supernovas. Black screens that filled with light and then went black again. A week before, the offices had been filled with people riding the crest, the buzz that said this new wave was endless; only fools thought otherwise. Meanwhile, somewhere at the center of the universe, stars were collapsing, matter was being sucked back toward the moment of creation, and the whole thing was getting ready to start all over. Dante saw the weary, dead look in Solano's eyes.

"You are kind of in a bind here. You turn on your friend Smith, and they'll abandon you. But you protect him—and you'll be convicted."

It was a strategy he'd often used in interrogations. Show the suspect he was cornered on both sides—then give him an avenue of escape. Except he hadn't really given Solano a way out. Not yet. He wanted to push him deeper into the corner.

"I'm going to the cops," Dante said.

The truth was Dante had nothing. He had no proof. There was no computer disk, and the hired hands were all dead. But he didn't care. He could see Solano dissembling, and that was all that mattered. He didn't care about justice anymore. All he wanted was to see that look in Solano's eye when it all came unhinged. Dante turned to leave. The big bluff. Behind him, he heard Solano rummaging in his desk.

"Wait a minute," said Solano.

Dante turned. Solano was holding a revolver. Dante glanced from the gun to Solano, and saw on his expression the fecklessness, the inner despair, the confusion Dante had always suspected was there beneath the surface, but at the same time he saw the boyish good looks and that vaporous smile that had so endeared the man to Angie.

"Come here," said Solano.

Dante didn't move.

"Come on," said Solano. "I have something I want to show you."

Dante knew about moments like this. He had studied them in criminology class once upon a time and experienced a few up close. The moment when a desperate man was cornered, he could do anything. You had to offer him hope. Otherwise . . . But Dante didn't want to offer Solano hope.

Solano smiled then, an ugly, funny smile, an echo of itself, stripped of its charm. Dante gave him the same smile back. Then Solano raised the gun and put the barrel into his mouth.

There was a spray of red and Solano fell to the ground. He fell in a heap. No one came running. They were too busy looting the building. Dante considered calling the cops, but decided not to.

Let him lie there. Let the cops find him on their own.

EPILOGUE

Dante left the old cannery and headed down Jackson to Columbus Avenue. This was the old business district, down in the hollows, where the Italian *prominenti* had had their offices. There were cottages back in the alleys, steel overhead. At the corner, a shaft of light. Then shadow. Up ahead, the Pyramid was lost in vapor. Dante could smell the vanished meadow beneath the concrete; he could smell its mud stench and hear the larks singing in the dunes that were no longer there. He headed up the hill, up the stone path, along Columbus. Out in front of Tosca's, a fishmonger pushed his cart into traffic. The doors of the Hungry-I were open, and the big notes of a tenor sax rippled the street. On Telegraph Hill, above the ramshackle little houses, goats were running loose, and a telegraph operator sat hunched in the wind. Everything was mixed together, all the layers. Gold seekers and railroad workers and wartime riveters stumbled off the docks to peer up a local girl who sat with her legs spread inside the Naked Moon. Dante looked, too.

The dead mingled with the living. The fog dissipated. Returned. The sky was nothing but blue.

Dante kept along Columbus. It was a plank road, built after the neighborhood itself, angling across the old streets to connect the wharf to the warehouses on the North Shore. The tourists walked the planks, headed toward the Pyramid. The sirens wailed down Vallejo, out of Columbus Station. In a little while the cops would be standing over the corpse, but they would never put it together. There were no paths back to La Rocca, Dante told himself. Just as there were none back to Smith. It always worked that way, and it made him wonder, if men like them, those two, if they were one and the same.

Protected by the devil himself, as Grandmother Pellicano might say. By the vindictiveness of men.

He kept walking.

Up here was Washington Square, the Cathedral of Saints Peter and Paul. Over there, the bench where he and Angie had sat once upon a time; and over there, the steps where the communion picture had been taken. There was another family there now, and Antonelli and his grandfather and the others mingled with them on the sidewalk. On the corner was a sawhorse with a sign on it and an arrow pointing uphill.

Open House

1547 Weber

Prospero Realty

Dante followed the arrow. On the way he passed a couple holding hands. A disconsolate man in a beret. A Chinese boy and his ancient grandmother, whose history in the city, Dante figured, went further back than his own. There was a cop all in blue, who gave him the nod, and then Dante turned the corner.

Marinetti's place.

Dante walked up the stairs. The same stairs Marinetti had come up the day he'd gotten married, and the same stairs the twins had descended on the night they died on Ocean Highway.

Don't forget us.

The place did not have quite the look it had the week before. It was decorated pretty much the same, in the same clean-edged style, with the pictures of Marinetti's family tucked away, and bright new pillows piled high on the bed, and artificial flowers in mauve vases. Only now Dante could sense the old man's presence. Cigar smoke. A wine bottle on top of the refrigerator, half empty. A crossword puzzle underneath the coffee table.

Also the crowd was gone. It was just Marilyn now, on the phone, alone on the couch. It took him a minute, but then he realized she was talking to the Widow Bolinni, who was a million years old and owned a fourplex down at the end of Fresno, not far from his father's place. She rented it out, and Prospero did the management. Marilyn hung up.

"What's the matter?" asked Dante.

"Raccoons," said Marilyn.

"Raccoons?"

"That's what the old woman says. Her son was out there with a flashlight, and saw one shimmy up the drainpipe. They're nesting up in the attics, crawling building to building. Mrs. Bolinni caught one, apparently, shredding her mother's wedding gown."

Dante thought of the animal smell in his mother's attic. He thought of the boxes that had been knocked over and the things that had been strewn around.

"Where's the crowd?"

"They backed out."

"Who?"

"The buyer. They backed out of the deal."

"Luckily—you've got the other offers."

"Nothing in writing. And the way things sit now, well, we're chasing the market down."

"What do you mean?"

"Things have shifted."

He looked at her then—her just graying hair, her rayon blouse, her jewelry, her makeup that seemed a little too heavy for the afternoon light—and when she moved away from him, all the hesitation he'd felt suddenly turned into resolve, into desire.

"I have to call someone," she said.

She stepped into the other room, where Marinetti's bed was stacked high with those pillows, and Dante thought about the man in gray. She did not close the door, and he could hear her talking.

"I just wanted you to know," she said. "We're accepting offers."

Her voice had a certain enthusiasm, and vulnerability as well, and Dante realized the balloon had popped. The boom was over. Likely, the truth was Marinetti had a second mortgage on the place already. Then there was the cost of the retirement home to think about, and the real estate commission, and back taxes. Not to mention the money his daughter and her husband were going to need. The sale price would be high, maybe, but not as high as they needed, and the margins were narrow.

A young couple entered the flat, whether potential buyers or lookie-lous, it was hard to know. They glanced Dante up and down, mistaking him for an agent, it seemed, one of lower reputation. A few days ago, the people who came to look, they had been all anticipation. But this couple's demeanor suggested they could take it or leave it; they were neither particularly impressed nor easily pleased.

"Is there a view?" the woman asked.

Dante nodded toward the kitchen.

"The ad said quaint," she said. "The ad said Old World."

The husband smirked. He wandered over to the table that Marilyn had laid out for the visitors and ate a cookie.

"Is this the first open?"

"It was last week."

"Not so many people today."

"Not at the moment."

"Any offers?"

"There's been a lot of interest."

The wife regarded the refreshment table. "I would have thought there'd be wine."

"I'll remember that for next time."

"The view?"

"Out there," he said, nodding toward the kitchen. "On the porch. You can see a long ways."

The couple stepped out onto the landing, but he could tell they didn't understand. All they could see was the laundry line and the stairs descending to a dark patio where the garbage was stacked up below.

But it was true.

You could see everything from here. You could see all of North Beach. You could see the Sicilians in their boats way out to sea. You could see the old shoals where the Calabrian hags beat their wash against the rocks.

You could see all the way to Singapore. To the Abruzzi Mountains. To goddamn fucking Cleveland.

The couple shook their heads, but they lingered a while anyway, eating cookies and drinking soda. They walked around the living room. They inspected the bath and peered into the bedrooms. Finally they went the way they had come, and Dante heard them clumping down the stairs. Outside, the light was changing. It was a light like you saw along the California coast in the early evening, with the tide rushing out, the waves receding. The boom was over, but the people were still here, and they weren't going to leave. No. It was the double trap, the two-way fix. Prices would go up, but there would be no jobs. There would be money, but not for you, not for me. Another wave crashed along the shore and the light grew yellow.

Marilyn stood beside him. Dante put his arms around her. The truth was, you couldn't save anyone, and no one could save you.

He kissed her. She kissed him back. They disentangled. Outside the dead were beckoning.